Kayfabe
& Other Stories

Kayfabe

& Other Stories

By Saul Lemerond

One Wet Shoe Publishing 2013

© Copyright 2013 by Saul Lemerond

Published by   One Wet Shoe Publishing
1709 W. Lyons St
Mount Pleasant, MI 48858
www.onewetshoe.com

ISBN 978-0-989607-10-0

ACKNOWLEDGMENTS

"Fake Barry" was originally published by *Greatest Lakes Review*, "Sid's Motor Bar" was originally published in *The Waterhouse Review*, and "White Fields and Emerson," was originally published in *Notes Magazine*. There are several (altered and unaltered) quotes from both Ralph Waldo Emerson and Henry David Thoreau in "White Fields and Emerson."

I'd like to thank all of my friends, family, mentors, and colleagues whose advice, patience, love, and support have made this collection possible. Their number is great, and they are too numerous to list here, but I'm certain they all know who they are, and I'm grateful to all of them. I'd especially like to thank Matt Richardson, who graciously accepted my request to illustrate the cover for this collection.

Cover art by Matt Richardson. Cover design, layout, and typesetting by Amee Schmidt. Titles in Optima and text in Georgia. Author photo courtesy of Michelle Campbell.

Contents

Fake Barry	5
Sid's Motor Bar	23
Cowboys in Rainbow City	31
Kayfabe	73
White Fields and Emerson	89
Reptiles in Tijuana	97

This is dedicated to my partner and continued source of inspiration, Valerie Johnson.

Fake Barry

There is a beautiful woman in my kitchen who says she's my mother, and she's not. I find this strange.

When I was younger, strange things never happened to me. Back then, my life was uncomplicated. My mother was my mother and everything was much, much simpler. When I was eleven, on most nights after dinner, I would sit down on the couch in the living room with my mother and watch TV. I would always be on one side of the couch with my tiny boy-feet stretched toward the center pillow, and my mother on the opposite side with her feet stretched towards mine. With the two of us positioned like this, and with me being a child and my mom being the woman she was, a game of footsy was always inevitable. We would sit under the glow of the TV, mingling our toes and tickling each other's feet.

I think of these nights fondly. There was always a softness in my mother's eyes and a warmth to her body. Sometimes, I wonder if this is where my attraction to older women came from. She always gave me a good feeling, and I always felt safe around her.

I suppose I think of these things now because, as I said, there is a woman in my kitchen who claims to be my mother, a woman who isn't my mother and seems to be having a difficult time accepting the fact that she's not. I know my mother when I see her, and this ain't her. This woman is an impostor, a faker, a stranger standing in my kitchen and crying for reasons I don't understand. Though, I must admit, she is kind of cute.

"You're in the wrong house," I tell her. "You walked into the wrong house. I'm not your son, but if you tell me your son's name, maybe I can help you find him."

"This isn't the right house," she admits, looking around a bit befuddled but then locking her striking sky-blue eyes with mine, "but you are my son."

She seems quite sure of this as she slowly looks me up and down. I say nothing.

"Barry?" she says haltingly. She looks like a child who has just learned there is no such thing as Elmo. "Don't... don't you recognize your mother?"

Her crying is steadily increasing. I wish this was a date and not a case of mistaken identity. Do people this beautiful always come with this much baggage?

"Look," I say, trying to phrase my response in a way that will not make her erupt like a volcano of emotional pressure. "I don't know who you are."

This doesn't create the desired effect.

"Barry!" she screams. Her eyes are beet-red and the wrinkles on her face become troughs for rivers of her tears. "Why are you doing this to me?"

Fake Barry

She runs toward me, and I grasp her wrists before she can grab hold of me.

"Please," she pleads. "I love you."

The only thing I can think to say is, "I'm sorry."

She screams again, and her face turns up a shade of red, then her eyes go blank, and she faints dead away. I already have a firm grip on her and do my best to keep her from crashing onto my tile floor. I carry her to my living room, turn on the lamp, and lay the unconscious woman on the lounger.

I must admit, there is a resemblance. She's right around the same age as my mother, probably a young forty-nine. She has the same wavy blonde hair and cute stubby nose. She has my mother's figure, the figure of a woman who gave birth once at nineteen and then worked hard to make sure no one could tell. Has her fashion sense too; the flower print red dress that flatters her hips and waist is certainly something she'd wear.

She's not my mother, though. I have no urge to tickle this woman's feet, and there are several things she's got that my mother doesn't. For one, she's more attractive. There seems to be sort of a glow about her; a sexy glow, almost playfully sexy. It's the kind of sexy I like. My own mother was never sexy. I am absolutely certain of this.

I give calling the police a moment's thought but decide against it. She seems harmless enough. Plus, lately, it has been rare for a beautiful woman to stay over.

***

I hate my job.

Click

The clock on the office wall always reminds me of the clocks we had in my house as a kid.

"Hello, Ms. Phillips, my name is Barry. I'm calling on behalf of ComPlex. We have an exciting new offer..." *Click*

It's one of those traditional clocks with twelve numbers and three hands. I have no idea why the hell they even make them anymore.

"Hello, may I please speak to Stanley Johnson? Hello, Mr. Johnson, my name is Barry from ComPlex and I'm offering a two-month free..." *Click*

"And a beautiful day to you, Ms. Perchfield. I'm calling on behalf of..." *Click*

Sometimes, when it's dead quiet, I hear the thing tick off the seconds of my life.

"Hello, this is Barry from..." *Click* Tick, tick.

It's almost as if I can make out the rhythm of my sorry existence.

"Hello?" *Click* Tick, tick.

"If I could have just a moment of your time?" *Click* Tick, tick.

"I represent..."

Tick, tick.

I try to ease my own atmosphere by talking to folks after they hang up on me.

"Good evening to you, sir. Did you know that..." *Click* "...And did you know I'm letting a strange woman who thinks she's my mother stay in my house?"

Click "She won't leave."

Click "I don't even know if I want her to leave... she's kind of cute."

"Oh, god, it's been such a long time since I've gotten laid. Is it wrong that I think a woman who kind of looks like my mother is attractive?"

"What?!" The voice of a customer comes through into my ear piece.

Oops, lost my rhythm.

"Oh, I apologize, Ms...Thomson. My name is Barry, and I'm calli..." *Click*

I woke up this morning to the smell of coffee and homemade French toast. I walked into the kitchen, and she was making me breakfast, standing right around the spot where she had fainted the night before.

"I'm sorry," I said, "but I don't know you. I think it would probably be better if you left."

At this, she began to cry again, but it was different this time, not hysterical like before. She put her head down and cried silently to herself.

In the daylight, she didn't look as crazy as she had the night before. Instead, she just looked sad, deeply sad, and I was touched in a way that made me feel as though I had, up to this point, been a complete asshole.

"Look," I said. "Can I get you some help? Give you a ride home or maybe call someone for you?" She tried wiping her tears with a dishtowel but they were just replaced by more.

"I have nowhere to go," she whispered, "and no one to call. You're the only one I have." Then she looked at me like I was the last person left on the planet and said, "I love you, Barry."

This broke my heart. Here was a woman who needed my help. A beautiful, lively, vivacious woman who needed my help and here I was trying to push her out my door. I felt ashamed for making such a beautiful creature sad, so I let her stay under the condition that we would have to have a serious talk when I got home from work, which brings me to back my job.

I hate my job. Even when there is not a gorgeous, crazy woman in my house, I hate my job. People hang up on me all day, and I'm pretty sure no one at the office likes me.

"Hello, my name is Barry. I'm calling on behalf of ComPlex, where quality custom copiers are our specialty..." *Click*

When I first started here, I'm pretty sure I actually liked myself, thought that I was a good person, and that my existence held some sort of inherent value. This translated into a confidence that allowed me to pick up women and then engage them in good conversation that would make them like me.

Situations like this are no longer an option. Although I am relatively good at my job, it does not change the fact that it is still a daily exercise in humiliation and rejection. When these things go on long enough, they both start to become something you expect out of life.

I still have hope, though, and I think that's why my coworkers hate me. It seems to me they abandoned hope a long time ago and find it ridiculous that I haven't, and because of this, they sometimes go out of their way to try and get under my skin.

Fake Barry

Like today for instance, when I came in to find that they had replaced my old desk with another old desk. I suspect Bob or Fred. Neither of them had said anything to me the entire time I've worked here and are always making it obvious that they don't like me. Replacing my desk with another, similar desk must be their odd way of getting their jollies, as I've been complaining that I need a new desk for just over two years, and here they are giving me another old desk. They even took the time to find a used desk that looks a lot like my original one. It even has a chip in the right-hand corner like the old one did. In fact, looking at it now, I'd say it looks more like the old one than the old one did.

This wouldn't bother me as much except that I'm sure most of the women who work here don't like me much, either. In fact, thinking about it now, this is probably the reason why I'm letting a crazy woman stay in my house. I think it's nice to have the female company. Probably, it's also because she's incredibly attractive, and I have a thing for incredibly attractive women.

"Ma'am, your ComPlex copies will be of such high quality they'll look better than the originals..." *Click*

I bet the cute crazy woman will have a good dinner ready for me for when I get home. I kind of hope she does; the French toast this morning was a nice change. Maybe I should try to keep her around. Sure, she seems a bit crazy, but I tend to be attracted to that sort of thing, too. Plus, doesn't everybody have problems? If I went around rejecting everyone who had some kind of problem, I wouldn't stand a chance of having anyone.

It's a simple case of mistaken identity. Maybe it's something we can work on together. I like her, and she could like me if she could get it through her head that

I'm not her son. I think this might have the makings of a wonderfully productive relationship. If not, well, then we both got problems, and how is that different from anyone else, anyway?

"How can a copy be better than the original, you ask?" *Click* Tick, tick.

***

I walk in the door, and she has dinner ready for me like I had hoped. She's made meatloaf—beautiful, wonderful—meatloaf.

"Smells delicious," I say, sitting down and grabbing a fork. Maybe it's the food, but she looks even more beautiful than I remember.

She stares at me for a long moment, inspecting me like a piece of fruit with some minor flaws on its rind. I'm not bothered by this and happily shovel meatloaf into my mouth. It has been a long time since anyone this attractive has shown me any attention.

"This is really good," I say, pointing my fork at the meatloaf.

"Thank you," she says, still eyeing me in such a way that I start to feel as though I may have done something wrong. Again, I'm not too bothered by it. There is something about her that I find almost irresistible. I find myself needing her and having to tell her so, but explaining to her that I am not her son seems like a very hard task.

I'm beginning to speak when she says, "You're not my son."

I look up from my meatloaf. "What?"

Fake Barry

"You're not my son," she says again, and I'd be happy but she sounds accusatory. Her eyes turn red, her face turns ugly, and she points an index finger at me slowly saying, "You're...not...my...."

As much as I don't want to, I abandon my meatloaf.

"Wait," I say, stopping her. "Don't you see this is a good thing? I like you, and I want to take care of you." I look her in the eye and smile my best 'I want you' smile.

"But," she whispers, her face softening again, "my son..."

"You can stay here," I tell her, motioning to the rest of my house. "We can make this work. I think you're beautiful, and I want to help you. I'll do anything you want. Get you whatever you need. I make good money. I'll even help you find your son."

She looks at the tiles of my floor.

"But," she says pointedly, "you're a faker."

"No, I'm not a faker," I say, "I want you to understand what you do to me. I need..." I stop myself as I notice she has the unmistakable look of an unsatisfied woman who wants to run out of my house.

A moment later, she turns and runs toward the living room. I run after her, but she has too much of a head start. I hear the front door slam shut and, by the time I open it, my beauty has disappeared into the night.

I go back to the kitchen, sit down to her meatloaf, and wonder if she's coming back. Looking down at my fork, I realize it's not my fork, though it looks remarkably similar. Why'd that hot mess bring her silverware into my home?

***

I wake up, hear the doorbell, get out of bed, and go see who it is. She's at my door and looks terrible. Her face is swollen, tiny purple veins spider web the whites of her eyes, her flower print dress is dirty and wet, and she's shivering from the cold. I grab a blanket and wrap it around her. She grabs me. I hold her so close I can feel her warm breath on my neck, and I'm excited.

"I don't know what to think," she says, looking at my coat rack, confused and vulnerable.

I put a finger to her lips and then kiss her, fully and deeply. She tries to pull away, but I don't let her. After a couple of seconds, her body relents and she kisses me back, and a warm buzz floods out from my chest and out through my extremities. The moment of electricity lasts as long as I've heard moments like this should. Time crawls like a snail in a garden, I let her go. There is a softness in her eyes and a openness to the glow of her body, and everything's going to be all right.

"We need to get some rest," I tell her, and show her to my bedroom.

***

I do not hate my job so much. Even if they have replaced the old analogue three-hand clock with a clock that is also old and analogue and three-handed. One that also ticks. One exactly the same as the old one.

I don't let it get to me. I have a beautiful woman, and it feels good. It's been too long.

A man taps me on the shoulder. It's Bob; he works in the cubical next to me. His well-manicured hand holds a black pen in my face, and he proceeds to speak

Fake Barry

the first words he's ever spoken to me in our three years together at the company.

"This isn't my pen," he says. "I know my pen when I see it, and this ain't it. Did you take my pen and replace it with this one?"

"Why would I do something like that?"

Anger swells in the lines around Bob's eyes.

"I don't know," he says. "Why don't you tell me?"

"I don't know anything about your pen," I say. "Besides, what does it matter as long as it works?" I ask, "Does it work?"

"It works fine," says Bob, "but that's not the point. I want to know what happened to my pen. I want to know what sick bastard would take my pen and replace it with a different pen." His excitement takes the form of small drops of spittle flying from his mouth and landing on my shirt. "You trying to play tricks on me, Barry?"

With my new woman in mind, I smile and say, "Screw the pen, Bob."

"Hey!" another voice rises from the cubical next to ours. It's Fred, another coworker who has neglected to speak a word to me since he started working here sixteen months ago, "Shut up! At least you woke up in your own house!"

"What?" asks Bob, absentmindedly placing his pen in his front pocket.

"When I woke up this morning, someone had replaced my house with a different house."

"A different house?" asks Bob.

"Yeah," says Fred. "It looks like my house, but it's not. I know my house when I see it."

"How the hell could that happen?" I say.

"I don't know," he says. "I'm wondering if maybe Bob did it."

This makes me laugh.

"Hey!" This voice was from our supervisor coming from around the corner. "I don't know who the hell you people are, but if you don't start doing the jobs you come here to pretend to do, you're all fired!"

***

When I was younger, strange things didn't happen to me.

"Hello, my name is Barry. I'm calling on behalf of ComPlex."

"You're not Barry." The man over the phone seems pretty sure of this. "I know a Barry when I hear one."

"You couldn't possibly know that," I say. "You've never met me."

"Look, whatever your name is. If you're going to lie about your name, then how can you expect me to trust that you're being honest about anything else?"

"My name doesn't matter," I say. "What does matter is how we at ComPlex are able to sell copy machines that make copies of such quality that you'll think they're better..." *Click*

This has been happening all day. I don't understand these people. If I'm someone else, does the customer still not get the same terrific offer? Do they not get the same first two months free? Do they not get ComPlex's excellent service plan? I know for a fact that I am me, but what the hell should they care if I'm me or not? It's not like my boss cared earlier today when I talked to him. Perhaps it didn't help that he called me in on a bad day.

"You're not the one I want," he said when I walked into his office. "I wanted Barry." He picked up a piece of paper off his desk and waved it at me. "Every performance review on this floor is absolutely terrible, but I'm going to have to say his are by far the worst of the bunch. Could you go back out there and send Barry in here for me, please?"

This confused me, as I'm the only person here named Barry.

"You wanted Barry," I said.

His eyes turned to slits, "I do want Barry."

My eyes opened wide, "I am Barry."

"You don't look like Barry."

"I can assure you that I am." My boss looked at me and then down at his paper again for more than a few moments, getting frustrated after obviously not finding what he was looking for.

"I don't care if you're Jesus Christ!" he yelled. Spit sprayed from his lips, and he again waved his piece of paper at me that did not look like my performance review. "Not with performance reviews like this one. We sell copiers here. Do you understand that?"

"High quality copiers," I nodded in agreement with slight confidence.

"They practically sell themselves," added my boss, still waving the sheet of paper he said was a performance review.

"Copies better than the originals," I mentioned the slogan, almost automatically.

My boss seemed somewhat placated by this and set the paper back down on his desk, saying, "You need to shape up or you're gone, do you understand me?"

I nodded again, and he motioned toward the door. As I walked out his office, I heard him yell, "And if you see Barry out there, tell him to give Bob his pen back!"

If I was still alone in this world, days like today might bother me. But I'm not alone. I have a woman at home who wants me, who will do anything for me, who has confessed to me that I am the most passionate lover she has ever had.

The day before yesterday, I drove home on a street that had just that day been replaced by a new street that, for all intents and purposes, looked just like the old one. I did this in a car that wasn't mine, though luckily there was a key on my keychain that worked in its ignition. I wondered if I should be concerned about my car and mentioned it to my lover.

"It doesn't matter, Barry," she said, pressing her body against mine, "as long as we love each other."

Then I kissed her, and we made love, once in the kitchen, then again in the bedroom. We lay awake in bed all night, caressing each other's bodies and gazing into each other's eyes.

We were in the living room when I said, "I love you," and tickled the sides of her belly. She screamed, I laughed, we fell off the couch, and she started tickling my feet.

I went to tickle hers and found her feet had been replaced with someone else's, but the feet were still beautiful, so I tickled them anyway, laughing as she laughed.

Sid's Motor Bar

Had the cue ball at Sid's Motor Bar the capacity to think, it might have wondered how it came to rest on the desert of green felt that had become, with few exceptions, its permanent home. The cue ball didn't mind it there. It was treated well. There was a single light bulb illuminating the pool table and it reflected sexily, like a small sun, off the ball's polished surface. The cue ball appreciated this greatly and believed this to be its most enticing characteristic. It had happily spent many a glorious afternoon at the center of all bar attention, but today was a sad day, for the only cue stick in the bar was being broken over the head of a man named Simon.

"No more games tonight," the ball remarked, low in tone. "No one's probably going to clean that blood off the felt, either."

* * *

Simon had two goals for his day. He'd been looking for love and trying to avoid getting arrested. He wasn't having a good month, nor had he had many good months previous. There had been too little love, far too many arrests, and copious amounts of other problems. It was not as though Simon was a bad person who deserved no love and constant arrest. It was just that his personality had some faults, probably the biggest of these being the syphilis he'd contracted (but would not admit to having).

The syphilis had come to him fifteen years earlier by way of a lady named Nadine who thought his curly blond hair was cute and, at the time, wanted to get laid by a man who would not bother her after she told him, post coitus, to go away. A man who would, for one night, do whatever she asked, whenever she asked, without question. Nadine approached Simon at a bar and told him that he was such a man. She told him that she would give him a precious gift. Simon had thought the gift she had to give him was love. It wasn't. That night, Nadine gave Simon the precious gift of syphilis.

Over fifteen year's time, Simon's asymptomatic, brain-eating, venereal disease had done so much damage that his brain had finally begun to run out of ways to compensate for its slow disintegration. The denial had been strong and the neurological trauma had been slow. Simon and his brain now suffered from four distinct delusions:

1. He was accepting his own reverse reasoning: A good example of reverse reasoning would be like thinking your mood affects the weather, when more than likely it's the weather that affects your mood. Or, it's like thinking you don't have syphilis because you feel fine, when more than likely you think you feel fine because you're in denial about having syphilis.

2. He believed love to be the solution to all his problems. Admittedly, there is a sense in which this delusion is ubiquitous in society. Most probably, it's due to the fact there are many ways in which love helps people become psychologically better suited to deal with their existing problems. It has been scientifically proven, however, that syphilis is resistant to even the strongest, most powerful feelings of love. If someone has syphilis and is faced with a treatment of love or penicillin, they would be wise to choose the penicillin.

3. Simon sometimes would confuse inanimate objects for sentient beings, capable of both love and sexual desire: Simon, like so many of us, conflates the action of sex with the feeling of love. This is particularly sad for Simon because there is a sense in which loving objects "in public" invites arrest from the police.

4. The idea that remained in his mind of Nadine had, for Simon, become the very personification of love, and he believed that anything that reminded him of Nadine was most certainly a path to the love he desired.

So, again, looking for love on a mostly cloudy day, Simon decided to stop in at Sid's Motor Bar because he could have sworn he saw Nadine or someone who resembled Nadine, which was just as good. He learned that he was wrong about the possibility of Nadine likenesses when he entered the bar, but regardless, the fact that the bar contained potential lovers could not be denied. He went inside, sat down at the bar, and ordered a drink. He then noticed a sexy glint of light coming from the direction of the pool table. Upon closer inspection, he found the source of sexy light was, in fact, coming from the cue ball.

He put on his best smile. "Hey there, sexy," said Simon to the cue ball.

"Hello," replied the cue ball in a sultry voice, low in tone.

Simon quickly decided to convince this most magnificent specimen of shiny cue ball into leaving the bar, going to his place, and jumping into the sack with him. He sauntered over to the pool table, looking shy enough to seem coy, but not so shy as to appear insecure.

Things began smoothly; Simon's courting of the sexy ball began in the most casual of ways, but he let himself get too excited and quickly digressed into proposals sexually perverse in nature. All smoothness was lost. A pool cue was heard breaking and blood found itself racing out from Simon's unfortunate head.

Then Simon's feet left the ground and his body was flying, some would even say gracefully, through the air. Why some might describe this flight as "graceful" is irrelevant. The important thing to know is this strangely idyllic parabola of flight ended in the gravel parking lot. All that beautiful momentum dispersed amongst thousands of bits of rock.

One mightn't wonder the cause of this violence. Well. If at any moment while propositioning the sex, Simon had thought to look past the cue ball; he'd have noticed a woman standing on the opposite end of the pool table with a look on her face that in no way resembled amusement, or gentle acceptance, or humored resignation, or polite supplication, or anything but a complete look of disgust. The sight of which, her boyfriend, Piston Pete, regularly used for kicking ass in bars.

Sid's Motor Bar

Once out in the gravel parking lot, Simon was startled by what had quickly become a foggy, rainy day. Though, really, it was neither foggy nor rainy; the experience being an interesting effect of blood dripping down into his eyes from a gash in his head. Simon's eyes focused and unfocused; so did his consciousness.

When he'd finally regained full use of his senses, he found himself alone and unloved again. He wondered briefly of himself and cue ball and their short but sultry liaison. He was saddened by its violent end and disturbed by his own altered kinesthesia. At least there were no police. It is hard to find love when one is under arrest. It is harder still when the officers spray pepper spray into the eyes before doing the arresting.

Simon walked to the back of the bar and peered in its back window. The billiard table was empty, and the cue ball rested on the bloodied felt as sensually as ever. He opened the back door, grabbed the ball, ran out, and confidently strode down the sidewalk as if nothing had happened.

"Do you think you might like to come back to my place?" asked Simon. The sunlight reflecting off the cue ball made it look as if the white sphere was smiling. Simon wondered if this could be love.

"I'm wondering what your name is," he said.

"Nadine," replied the cue ball, low in tone.

Cowboys in Rainbow City

The sky is full of rainbows. Shelly, a seven-year-old girl, sits next to her teddy bear on the couch. In another room, her brother is coughing. Outside, a building explodes. Shelly pays no attention to the sound or to the small bits of debris from the four-story insurance building falling past her window, and neither does her teddy bear. This isn't entirely their fault: the couch they're sitting on is facing away from the window, and the show they're watching has shocked them, quite violently, into a rage trance.

The big screen shows a beautiful beach of white sand. The sun is shining, techno music is playing, and small waves roll up on the shore as young people dance.

"This is abhorrent." Shelly's head wobbles in horror. More than anything, she hopes her eyes might be lying to her.

"Disgusting," agrees Teddy the teddy bear, scratching his furry chin with a furry paw.

The youths gyrate to the beat of the music in swimsuits that utilize as little fabric as possible. Shelly feels her seven-year-old eye twitch, opens her mouth, and, head still wobbling, speaks as slowly and deliberately as she can, "What is this abomination?"

Teddy knows she knows what they're watching, but answers anyway. "I believe the kids call it 'freak dancing,'" he says, his front paws resting firmly atop his large and furry belly.

The show continues. Techno-pop music's playing, and all over the beach, there are young ladies and young men bending over and thrusting their posteriors into the welcoming pelvic regions of other young ladies and men. Usually, it's a young lady's posterior that is thrust into a young man's pelvic region. But sometimes this positioning is reversed, or is between a man and a man or a lady and a lady, or any combination thereof. In fact, the combination seems not to matter.

"Sometimes referred to as 'booty grinding,'" Teddy adds.

Both parties continually bounce up and down to the techno. They're sweating profusely; no doubt the result of the intense friction between their posterior and pelvic regions. The look on Shelly's face lets Teddy know she needs a drink. She watches him get up and walk toward the kitchen. As he disappears from view, she notices a cross-eyed kitten walking jerkily into the room. For a moment, this strange tabby looks as though it's going to block the view of her program; instead, it crashes headfirst into the wall.

"Cody!" Shelly yells. "Could you please keep your inbred kittens on your side of the apartment?"

Her twin brother stumbles in. The seven-year-old boy wears thick, square-rimmed glasses and a pair of tighty-whitey underpants. He coughs, coughs again, and then readjusts his glasses, as they are askew his head.

"Sorry," he mumbles as he picks up the mangy, inbred tabby kitten. He exits the room as quickly as possible, probably trying to get away before Shelly can say anything else. As usual, he's too slow.

"You're supposed to keep them in your room," she snaps.

"Whatever," comes back from around the corner, along with another cough. From the opposite direction comes Teddy. The stuffed bear walks up to the coffee table and sets down two lowball glasses, a bucket of ice, and a freshly opened bottle of Moldy Poison Black Label Whiskey.

"I don't want any ice," grumbles Shelly. "Cowboy Rick doesn't take ice with his Moldy Poison."

Outside, another building explodes. Rubble from the five-story walk-up flies high up in the air before the arms of gravity bring it all back down. Again, debris showers the world beyond Shelly's window. Again, she doesn't notice. She takes a sip from her lowball. The kick from the pure liquor makes her head wobble noticeably.

She thinks about her show and her day, which is ruined because her favorite show has been cancelled. Probably, she would never see Cowboy Rick again.

The seven-year-old has been watching *Cowboys* for most of her life. The reality TV series chronicled the movements and exploits of several cowboys. Initially, Shelly was surprised by how little she knew about them as she figured them a plain and simple folk with a disposition for fist-fighting which, for the most part, was true—at least at first.

In the beginning, most of the show's conflicts centered on whether the cowboys were manly and prideful enough. An example being when one of the cowboys died in the "Rustlers Attacking the Cattle Drive" challenge and Cowboy Rick attributed Cowboy Dave's failure to shoot a single rustler as evidence of him "not being much of a man, much less a cowboy." The same could be said in the aftermath of the "Starving Settlers Attacking the Cattle Drive" challenge. Such incidents were common. Usually these episodes involved fistfights, which always did well in the ratings. But what really upped the ante and the viewership was when the host presented the cowboy cast with the "Creating Your Own Frontier Society" challenge: a society suitable to be known as truly "cowboy." Yes, indeed, this created many a fistfight, but just as interesting was how the different cowboys interpreted what it meant to be "cowboy." It made the show multidimensional, which Shelly liked. The fact that Cowboy Rick was extremely attractive was also something Shelly liked.

Had the show not been cancelled, "The Most 'Cowboy' Cowboy" challenge would have been set to air. This was a show where viewers would call in and vote on which cowboy they thought acted most like a real cowboy. Anyone who thought more than one cowboy fit the description then had to vote for who they thought was the realest cowboy.

Shelly had been waiting for "The Most 'Cowboy' Cowboy" challenge all week. There would be drama and politics, and most of all, there would be fistfights. She'd vote for Cowboy Rick, although she was pretty sure he'd win regardless. He was easily the most 'cowboy' of all the cowboys. He was rugged, dangerous, hard, and handsome. Over the years, Shelly had become very comfortable staring at Cowboy Rick and looked forward to having her esteem of him validated by the viewing audience.

But Shelly turned on the TV this morning to find that the show had been cancelled. And she now finds herself watching a show that's very much like most other shows. A show where real, live people who live by a real, live beach freak dance live to techno-pop music.

Thump, thump, thump goes the techno-pop. Shelly's head hurts. She flips through three channels. Each goes thump as she passes. She knows it doesn't matter, so she stops. There are one thousand channels; her brother Cody insists on having them. This results in the apartment now having access to one thousand different variations of freak dancing. It's on every channel; a reality show for every possible situation. Young people freak dancing on beaches and in clubs. Competitions for who is the best freak dancer. Booty-grinding for debt relief. Pelvic friction weight-loss expos. Celebrity freak dancing. It's even on newscasts.

Shelly swallows her drink. Teddy does the same, then refills their glasses.

"This has to stop," says Shelly, muting the television. "I mean, what would Cowboy Rick think of such debauchery?"

A vague thump, thump, thump, can still be heard from down the hall. The door to Cody's room is open. Two kittens, cross-eyed and drooling, exit Cody's bedroom, booty dancing past the living room on their way to the kitchen.

Teddy shakes his head, replies, "I couldn't agree more," and takes a drink.

Cody appears, still in his tighty-whiteys. He runs past the living room, presumably to retrieve his dancing kittens.

Shelly pretends she doesn't notice and continues her rant. "I mean, we don't just live anywhere; this is Rainbow City! We should be setting an example. Freak dancing is the kind of hedonism that will plunge us into amoral anarchy. With fine upstanding shows like *Cowboys* off the air, we're going to find ourselves on a crash course into the dark ages."

A voice comes from the hallway. "You know what your problem is?" Cody's voice startles Shelly. She looks up to find her brother at the entrance to the living room. In each hand, he's holding one of the two kittens who had booty danced past Shelly and Teddy just moments before.

"Your problem is you're too idealistic." He coughs, absentmindedly covering his mouth with one of his demented kittens, then says, "You think everyone has to think the same as you."

Shelly silently stares at Cody, who couldn't be more wrong. She just wants her show back. She wants Cowboy

Rick, her ruggedly handsome beefcake, back on the air and that's it. Not wanting to admit this to her brother, she instead points at the freak-dancing teens on the big screen.

"Is it too idealistic to want a program that doesn't consist entirely of pornography? When did continuous pelvis-to-butt contact become our chief form of entertainment?"

Cody frowns, and his kittens frown with him. "What're you going to do? Tell the kids 'no freak dancing?' They'll never listen to you. They're having too much fun."

Shelly shifts her gaze again to the gyrating youngsters grinding genitalia. The smiles are hard to miss. It would be difficult to argue fun wasn't being had.

"Look," she says, "I'm a good person. I pay my taxes. I volunteer time and give money to help the poor and needy because I love my city." Shelly empties her glass, thinking fondly of Cowboy Rick, the most 'cowboy' of all cowboys. "But the city I fell in love with was not trapped," Shelly's voice raises in anticipation of her final judgments, "in the sultry embrace of hedonism."

Whoops and hollers emit from the big screen while Shelly's big head shakes in anger. Teddy nods in agreement; with one hand, he's drinking and with the other, rubbing his furry belly.

Cody shakes his head. He's so excited that he forgets he's holding his kittens as he thrusts his right arm forward to gesture accusingly at his sister. "You're getting behind the times, Shelly. The world's passing you by."

The kitten stares at Shelly, or Teddy. It's hard to tell because of its crossed eyes. She ignores it. "Said the pot to the kettle," she indignantly replies to the boy who hasn't bothered to socialize with anyone except his kittens for a long, long time.

Cody keeps the one kitten thrust forward; it's no longer staring at Shelly but seems to be distracted by something debris-related going on outside the window. "Whatever, like cowboys even matter anymore."

"Hey, cowboys are relevant!" Shelly points sanctimoniously at the ceiling. "They help us better understand ourselves because they represent a microcosm of our social attitudes. Really, what could better express such things?"

Probably because he knows his sister is just repeating the opening monologue of the show, Cody says, "That's easy, watch this." He sets down his kittens and they immediately begin freak dancing. "How do you like that for attitude?"

Having made his point, Cody picks up his kittens and stalks off to his room. Shelly visualizes strangling her brother, and this makes her feel better momentarily. She doesn't understand why he's always so obstinate and wonders why he couldn't be more like Teddy. Now there's someone who knows how to agree with a person.

Looking over at him, she sees his furry paw pointed at the TV. It's a special report. The news camera's leveled at the city's central post office. There are, of course, several young people freak dancing out in front. They whoop and holler and rub and bounce, and behind them, the post office explodes.

Shelly un-mutes the TV. The announcer informs the viewing public of several similar reports there'd been over the course of that morning. Looking outside, Shelly and her bear find that their normally illustrious skyline is missing several buildings. Adjacent to their apartment window are a couple of smoking craters. Behind them, the announcer reports that Grandmaster Mayor Manley will be holding a town hall meeting to address the recent exploding building problem, after which he will allow the public to air grievances they have, if any. The ridiculously square jaw of the tremendously handsome Grandmaster Mayor now appears on screen.

Shelly always thought that if there were any man more manly than Cowboy Rick, it'd have to be Grandmaster Mayor Manley. This, of course, is the reason he gets elected over and over again. The man has a jaw people can't say no to.

She wondered what he would do about the exploding buildings; probably ban them. It's what he always does. Everyone in town knows if Mayor Manley thinks something's a problem, he bans it. For him, it's the simplest and most effective solution. When there were too many car accidents on the streets, he banned cars. When too many girls hurt their ankles playing hopscotch, he banned chalk. When he needed to appear tough on crime, he banned criminals. When he wanted to show his citizens they had nothing to fear from earthquakes, he banned earthquakes, and then he banned fear.

Thinking of all this creates an idea, the force of which makes Shelly's head shake harder than the kick from her Moldy Poison. If Grandmaster Mayor Manley could see freak dancing as a threat, he would ban it. The solution was as simple as that. He would ban freak dancing in all its forms, even the abstract ones, and freak dancing would be banned from television, and then it would only be a matter of time before Cowboy Rick was back on the air.

"We must go to that town hall meeting!" she shouts. Teddy gives her quizzical look, which she ignores. "Get our yellow rain coats, boots, and Cody's umbrella. I'll explain on the way!"

Teddy, who has always been a lightweight, is drunk. He stumbles to the hallway closet and retrieves two yellow raincoats, two pairs of green rubber boots, and Cody's enormous red and green striped umbrella. Getting ready to venture out into the city, they make sure to refresh their drinks and leave a note for Cody before they go.

***

On Cody's bed there is a pillow. Under the pillow is a gun. Next to the pillow and on top of the bed there is Cody. All around Cody there are kittens, because Cody is a kitty hoarder. And, in the immortal words of seven-year-old kitty hoarders everywhere: "It started out with just a couple of strays."

Although, most of the blame should be placed on his sister. Contrary to what one usually hears about twins, Cody's nothing like his sister and makes it his purpose to be so. It's not that he hates her; he doesn't hate her. He loves his sister. He's just never been anything like her and has no desire to be. Mostly, he finds her vain, close-minded, and grumpy. These, her undesirable characteristics, usually make him want to neutralize any negative effects she has on her surroundings.

The day he'd found those first strays had been mostly unremarkable. Cody and Shelly had just come home from the night-half of their swing shift at the rainbow factory. As always, work at the factory was grueling. It was when they took their usual route through the alley behind their apartment building that they noticed two stray kittens eating out of the trash.

"We should do something," said Cody, his heart melting.

"*Cowboys* is on, and I don't want to miss it," was the reply. She ignored the look of dismay on her brother's face and continued, "Just call Kitten Control. They'll take care of it," and went into the apartment building.

Cody pictured her plopping down on her couch with a glass of booze and her teddy bear, just in time to watch the first fist fight break out. He didn't like the show. He just didn't understand the appeal of watching two cowboys argue over what kind of immigration policy was more in line with the 'cowboy way.'

He did like kittens, though, and he knew there was little chance for them if he called Kitten Control, so he secreted them up to his room. Worried he might not be able to sneak them past Shelly and Teddy, he was relieved to find they were so completely focused on their show that he could have had a herd of kittens freak dancing their lives away in the next room, and they wouldn't have noticed.

So, while Shelly and Teddy watched Cowboy Steve explain how, "If we're going to let them live in our town, we should make them take a test, with both written and oral parts. Just so we knows they ain't cheatin', like most foreigners is like to do." Cody brought the strays to the kitchen and set down a bowl of milk for them.

The kittens had finished their meal and were playing in Cody's room by the time Cowboy Rick finished telling Cowboy Steve that if they needed to create tests for incoming citizens, then he needed to be punched in his stupid face for being so stupid.

Before work, Cody would lock the kittens in his room and no one was the wiser. Shelly and Teddy were usually too distracted or too drunk. By the time Shelly found out Cody was keeping the kittens, they'd already had a litter.

Initially, Shelly looked at the kittens with disdain, but she pitied her brother enough to not raise a fuss. Cody had no friends and his health was failing. Plus, she couldn't be bothered. Her days were filled with working, drinking, and watching *Cowboys* and *Cowboys* reruns. She ignored the kittens the first time she saw them because she was excited to tell Cody what was happening on *Cowboys*. And Cody, who was so happy his sister wasn't raising a fuss, actually listened to her explain to him how the cowboys were getting rich because they had developed a system to lend out cattle on credit and how that was the 'cowboy way.'

With the exception of the kittens sometimes wandering in front of her big screen television, she rarely complained about the members of his new kitten family.

And so it went. Every day, Shelly and Cody would come home from their ten-hour shift at the rainbow factory, Teddy would have a drink ready for Shelly, and Cody would go to his room.

While Shelly and Teddy were getting drunk and watching *Cowboys*, Cody and the rest of the kitty clan would be in his room, enjoying many channels of booty-grinding reality television.

It was not long before another litter of kittens came along. That litter reached maturity a short time later and also started having litters. Cody just loved his kittens. They were his family. He felt very much like a parent and wanted to treat them with as much love and care as possible.

Others, he knew, would probably point out how he was far too permissive in allowing them to inbreed. A more responsible kitten owner might have gotten them fixed in order to prevent such behavior. If ever asked, Cody would have been quick to counter that his wages were barely enough for him to pay rent, not to mention the ever-increasing cost of kitten food.

It is important to note that Cody was not and is not delusional. He knows he is a kitten hoarder. He's always been hypersensitive about his own behavior and has done his research. People who spent their careers studying kitten hoarding would gladly profile him as a typical obsessive-compulsive. Cody had previously felt alone but is now safe in the company of kittens who provide him with a support structure, a safety net, a cute and cuddly distraction from a harsh world that's slowly killing him.

It was nothing new. He'd always been nervous. He didn't like to be around people, didn't like to go outside, was afraid of uniformed police officers, and sometimes thought he was being watched. Every once in awhile, and for no apparent reason, he believed his molecules might be becoming unstable.

Life had not been good before his kittens. Aside from the slight amount of contact with his sister and a few other coworkers at the rainbow factory, Cody was alone. When he cried himself to sleep after his severe coughing fits, he was alone. When the doctor informed him the lung disease contracted from breathing in too much rainbow dust was terminal, he was alone. When he lied about his cough to others, he had never felt more alone. Worse was the fact that he did everything he could to convince himself it wasn't a problem, lying to himself as much as he did to other people.

Whenever Shelly showed concern about his cough, he'd tell her no, he was fine, and pretended like the rainbow dust he breathed in all day at the factory hadn't coated his lungs. His pulmonary constitution was ideal. He wasn't in pain, and it didn't matter if he was a little lonely. This was the way life was supposed to be, and everything was fine, just fine. He was most certainly not planning his suicide, and even if he was, he most certainly hadn't bought a gun and put it under his pillow for when he finally built up the courage to end all the suffering he most certainly wasn't in.

In retrospect, the day he'd rescued those first two kittens had been the happiest day ever. There was pure love in their eyes, and he knew taking them in was the right thing to do the instant he held them. He felt centered and fortified. These kittens loved him and wouldn't ever leave. He'd feed them, and they'd freak dance the evening away and then cuddle him to sleep. The feeling was intoxicating, and he felt alive for the first time in a long, long time. When he'd noticed that one of the stray kittens was pregnant, he wasn't bothered by the inbreeding. There would be more kittens now. What could possibly be wrong with that?

***

Shelly notices the Blue Street Bank explode off in the distance. She hands Teddy her drink and opens her brother's oversized red-and-blue-striped umbrella in preparation for incoming debris. Much to the gratitude of Teddy, the umbrella is large enough for both of them. Teddy thanks her for her consideration and hands her drink back, while brick and mortar are deflected away from them.

Teddy takes a fuzzy paw off his big belly and points to a rainbow arching over Blue Street, now visible because the bank is gone. "That yours?" he asks. "It's gotta be the most vivid one yet."

"Of course it is," she says flatly. "You know there's not a rainbow within leagues of here that didn't come from our factory."

Teddy does know. It is just that the reds, blues, and greens of this particular rainbow are quite fetching. "It's very beautiful."

Shelly, although appreciative of the attempt at conversation, ignores his comment. Instead she says, "I need a refill."

The bear hands her the bottle. The liquor is serving its purpose. Her nervousness at the prospect of confronting the Grandmaster Mayor becomes more and more subdued with each sip, as her courage and confidence are bolstered. How to convince Manley to put her show back on the air is troubling. The Grandmaster Mayor is a shrewd man. His is a jaw one does not question, for it comes bursting down from his skull commanding awe, respect, and obedience. Most folks requested nothing of him. Rarely did they question him, because if Manley didn't like something, he would've already changed it.

Looking up at the rainbow Teddy pointed out, she remembers standing on its red arch as it lay on the factory floor. Her job is to caulk the open space between the red and blue arches. Tedious work, no thought required. Over the years, the action has become as mindless as blinking, and the anticipation of seeing Cowboy Rick has gotten her through many a boring day. The absence of Cowboy Rick, she knows, will make her work unbearable.

Teddy says something, but she misses it. Before she can ask him to repeat himself, she's distracted by two men standing on a bridge in the distance, directly under her rainbow. She can barely believe her eyes.

"Cowboys!" she squeals in delight.

"What?" asks Teddy, drunkenly looking to see what she's on about. She points toward a bridge spanning the city's purple river. Upon this bridge, two cowboys stand next to a burlap sack. Shelly barely believes her luck. It's possible these two cowboys are the answer to her problems. The strength of the cowboy value system is something people admire, and with them, she just might be able to able to stand before the Grandmaster with a reasonable amount of confidence.

Teddy gives her a knowing look and strokes the hair on his belly. "What are you gonna say to them?" he asks.

"Yee haw, Teddy," the seven-year-old girl replies to her friend. "Yee haw."

***

Cody's television is on perpetual scan, and his kittens dance to their hearts' content. Every five or ten seconds, the television automatically switches channels. This seems the most pleasing setting for the kittens as they get varying stimulation in addition to uninterrupted freak dancing. Cody shakes as he coughs; it's getting worse again, but he's not worried. He's happy as long as his kittens are happy, and as long his kittens are booty dancing, they're happy. It's not like anybody ever got hurt because of booty dancing. Well, he supposed a lady with a lead butt could do him some damage, but such a thing was yet unheard of.

Apart from his kittens, there's extra satisfaction in the symbolism behind the craze. It was small at first, just a bunch of urban youths venting their anger at having to identify themselves with rainbows. Some had argued the first unhappy youths who embraced the movement would have been unhappy whether they had grown up in an industrial center like Rainbow City or not. Some people just couldn't let themselves be happy.

The fact that the movement grew so significantly in number and popularity was proof they'd been wrong. What began as just a fad, only embraced by the poorest and most destitute citizens of a large city center, had suddenly transformed into a full-blown cultural phenomenon, and, all at once, genitalia were being thrust about inappropriately at every turn.

Cody can't freak dance because of his rainbow lungs. He lives vicariously through his kittens as they vent their existential urban rage.

He leaves for the kitchen to get his kittens breakfast. Walking past the living room, he notices that Shelly and Teddy are gone. Their couch is empty, and Grandmaster Mayor Manley is on the big screen, shown standing in front of City Hall. He is tall and proud. It's obvious that several youngsters, who freak dance behind him as he speaks, are not supposed to be there.

Cody is not sure, but apparently there's some city emergency of sorts. It sounds like it may have something to do with some buildings exploding. The Grandmaster Mayor stands at his podium wearing his serious face. A significant amount of sunlight reflects off his jaw. He asks the viewers to please not panic. He promises to deal with this problem swiftly and with as little expense to the citizens of Rainbow City as possible. He currently has his best people working on it. There is a town hall meeting.

This reminds Cody of the sun fiasco the city had gone through a few years back. It was wintertime, and a bunch of folks complained how they weren't getting enough sun. It was all over the news. A rather vocal opposition spoke up, saying there wasn't supposed to be much sun in the winter, that that was one of the reasons why they called it winter, and why should they change such a storied institution like winter just because a few folks were getting depressed?

This sparked a great deal of debates. There were town hall meetings devoted to the topic, as well as televised debates that included social pundits and experts from the sciences discussing a possible banning of winter. In the end, nothing was done. Too many people liked skiing.

The skiers were, of course, expected to be sorry for inconveniencing everyone. It was all completely ridiculous, which is why Cody doesn't care for politics. All people do is complain, and in the end no one is happy.

He shuts down the screen and walks into the kitchen.

There's a note on the refrigerator:

> *Cody,*
>
> *Went to town hall to convince Mayor booty dancing must go. Be back later.*
>
> *Shelly*
>
> *P.S. Make sure no kittens in living room.*

The force of the letter hits Cody like a lead butt to the groin. The Mayor's power is absolute. If he wants freaking off the air, it's off the air. Sure, people might complain at first, but come election time, there won't a man or woman within leagues whose jaw even closely compares.

What the Mayor's reaction may be is impossible to tell. He has been too random, making capricious pronouncements that never favor any group. A decision on freak dancing could go either way. Cody can't have that. His kittens are the last good thing in his life, and their happiness is the only thing keeping him alive. His sister might not know it, but she's trying to murder him.

Cody marches into his room and retrieves his gun. The idea that he originally bought it to kill himself seems absurd to him now. There is too much to live for. He looks down at the chambers of his revolver. There are six bullets. Six bullets between him and the end of what the kids like to call 'the freaky grind.'

He puts on his red raincoat and green rubber boots, walks to the door, then stops. He'd almost forgotten his kittens still need tuna and milk. He gives it to them.

The gun in his pocket rattles against his keys as he walks out the door and then out onto Blue Street.

***

The cowboys look just like cowboys. They stand, wearing big thick brown boots, dirty blue jeans, and dusty leather chaps. They wear long leather coats with fringe on the sleeves and Stetson hats on their heads. Beneath their hats, their mustachioed faces are stern and weathered from constant exposure. A gun belt and large six-shot pistol hangs from both sides of each one's hips. Between them, a large, brown, lumpy, burlap sack.

The taller cowboy, the one closest to Shelly, turns his head and tips his hat in greeting.

"There somethin' I can do for you, little lady?"

Shelly, having never seen a cowboy in real life, is speechless. Standing mouth agape, face blushing, she ventures a side glace at Teddy, who is absentmindedly playing with the fur on his belly. Small hope of Teddy stepping in; the bear is an excellent listener but a horrible conversationalist. At the present moment, he is quite drunk, probably waiting for something to agree with.

The cowboys seem to have dealt with similar situations before. Because, after a moment of watching the awestruck Shelly stand before them, the tall one speaks to the short one.

"Kenny," he says, stretching his large fingers against his cowhide gloves. "What do you suppose this little girl and her teddy bear come all the way up to this here bridge for?"

"I reckon they's admirers, Boss," says Kenny, who, even though shorter than Boss, is just as rugged because his mustache is fuller and richer. "That there girl looks as though she might be a fan of cowboys, and the cowboy way." Kenny's face shines as he mentions this.

"I think you're right, Kenny. I think you're right." Boss wiggles his lesser, though still full and rich, mustache and points at the large burlap sack. "Then they're in luck because today they're gonna witness an authentic example of the cowboy experience."

"Love the show!" Shelly blurts out. Her face flushes red, and she quickly looks down at her glass. Teddy, empathizing with her pain, tops it off.

She starts to mumble an excuse, but Boss cuts her off. "Don't worry 'bout it. We're always happy when people take interest in the cowboy way." He turns and addresses his companion. "Ain't we, Kenny?"

"We sure is, Boss."

"We sure is," repeats Boss, nodding. He points at his sack. "This here might be the favorite pastime of quite a few cowboys, ain't it, Kenny?"

"It sure is, Boss," replies his companion.

"It sure is," repeats Boss.

Reaching into the sack, Boss pulls out a puppy. Judging by the floppiness of the pup's ears, it might be an English Cocker Spaniel. Shelly's only able to get a glimpse before Boss throws it over the side of the bridge. A small gasp escapes her lips as it goes over the rail. The puppy makes a small splash before the river's current takes it downstream.

Shelly runs to the guard rail and suddenly, she's deaf to everything. There's a loud ringing and she smells gunpowder. Kenny's pistol's drawn and smoking and back in the river, the puppy's disappeared. Shelly's confused.

Everything becomes clear when another puppy, this time a tiny golden retriever, flies over her head and plops in the water. The puppy's tiny blond head bobs down stream a bit until Kenny draws again. He fires three shots, and they wait for the smoke to clear.

Shelly's hearing returns, and there's a look on her face that resembles something less than amusement. Both cowboys seem to have anticipated her reaction.

"It would seem our little admirers are partial to golden retrievers," says Kenny.

"Do you mean to say, Kenny, that these two city slickers find fault with certain nuances of cowboy culture?"

Kenny spits and replies, "If I had to guess, I'd say it's the part where we throw the puppies into the river then shoot them dead, Boss."

"Why, but that's absurd, Kenny; you make it sound as though shooting puppies was like laughing in the face of God?"

"Well, Boss," Kenny answers, "I've heard tell that some folks take puppies, raise them to adulthood and glean a certain amount of satisfaction from their company. But, then again, most folks don't know nothin' 'bout art."

Before now, Shelly didn't believe cowboys could be so dramatic. But it was so obvious: cowboy culture meant cowboy art. These two men have come to this bridge to express themselves. Shelly and Teddy were now their audience.

"Well then, Kenny, what if I told 'em they sell big sacks like this one right next to the lead balls and black powder in the target shooting aisle at The Cowboy Warehouse?"

"Perhaps this little girl disagrees with that as well," says Kenny. "I myself have heard many a honest folk insist to me that puppies should not be shot, but petted. I've been told that it's why they call 'em pets."

"Pets?" asks Boss, playfully annoyed. "Why of course they are." Boss points at the side of the bag where the word "PETS" is printed in large, blocky, stenciled letters.

He picks out a red tick hound and gives it a toss. Kenny's six-shooter goes boom. He looks over to Shelly.

Another toss. Another boom. This time it's a chow-chow and Kenny lets out a whoop, his large Stetson hat shakes as he nods his approval.

"It's not just target practice you're seeing here. It's a transference of pain and lost innocence. That's the reason we came to the city today. We wanted to see if we could help people like you understand the reality of our lives."

If Kenny or Boss had direct access to Shelly's thoughts, they would've been quite taken aback by how much Shelly didn't care. Not only did Shelly care very little for the plight of cute puppies, she cared even less about cowboy performance pieces done in the name of truth, art, and politics. She cared not whether cowboys were correctly understood by a majority public. Nor did the plight she didn't care about become more highlighted when she watched them shoot puppies. Puppies were cute, yes, but Cowboy Rick was cuter, and she'd personally oversee the slaughter of all the puppies in Rainbow City if it meant she could get lost in his piercing blue eyes once more.

"Oh, I totally understand," says Shelly. "If you ask me, shooting puppies as a pastime is preferable to sitting on the couch and watching kids rub their asses on each other all day. It's obscene." Boss and Kenny frown at the mention of freak dancing, and she hopes she might be getting somewhere. "Personally, I like to drink. Teddy..." She looks at her bear, he hands her the bottle. She fills her glass and offers the bottle to the cowboys.

"I agree," says Boss, accepting the bottle. "I can't stand any o' them shows. They don't make no goddam sense. Absolutely no nuance."

"There's no depth to them," Kenny agrees, "and no meaning."

"Only good show left these days is *Cowboys*," says Boss. He takes the bottle from Kenny after he's finished.

"Oh, didn't you hear?" asks Shelly, taking the bottle. "They cancelled *Cowboys* and replaced it with *Beach Booty Dancing*."

The double travesty of this hits Boss and Kenny like a bullet hitting a puppy. Both men go silent and stare blankly.

"I know." Shelly's playing to them now. "I think it's a travesty. Why, me and Teddy here were just on our way to complain to Grandmaster Mayor Manley."

"I reckon we should...."

***

The Party Awning is rocking and the gun in his pocket rattles as Cody walks up Blue Street toward the town hall. His kittens are with him as well as about two dozen freak dancers. An entourage wasn't exactly what he had in mind when he'd left the house. Then, he'd been alone, on a solo mission to assassinate someone. If someone died, it would be his fault. The fact that he had an entourage would be his sister's.

Before Cody left his apartment, he had wondered why his sister had taken his umbrella. When bits of brick and mortar fell from the sky, his question was answered, and he was forced to take refuge in the first shop he came to. Thankfully, it was an umbrella shop. Sadly, there were no umbrellas. A question concerning this was on Cody's tongue when the manager came out from the back room.

"Sorry, but we're out of umbrellas." The manager was pale and looked as though everything confused him.

Cody was crestfallen; he could not let these exploding buildings stop him. "Look," he said. "I really need some sort of protection. You know, from all the falling debris. The quality of my life depends on it."

"Protection," the manager repeated confusedly, "from the debris. You mean something like an umbrella?"

Cody did not like where this was going. "Yes," he said, "like an umbrella."

Again, the manager looked confused. "We're out of umbrellas."

"I know," said Cody.

"Well," the manager appeared to look as though he was thinking very hard, "there is an armory store next door that sells all different sorts of shields. You know, like metal ones."

This couldn't have been more perfect, but before Cody could say so, the manager frowned and said, "But they're sold out too, I think."

Cody said nothing. The manager noticed this and again looked as though he was thinking very hard. "There's an awning store next to the armory. Business hasn't been too good for them lately, on account of there being a recent shortage of buildings. They'd probably be happy to sell you one."

"An awning?" asked Cody, dubiously.

"Yup, they're just like umbrellas but bigger. I imagine they could probably fix you up. They got cool designs and stuff."

The people at the awning shop were surprisingly helpful, but rainbow lung or no, awnings were simply too large for an individual to carry.

This is why Cody now has his kittens with him. He'd gone back and gotten them so they could help carry his awning, which from above, appears twenty feet in length and ten feet in width. At each corner of the awning there are eight kittens.

Four to help hold up a corner pole and freak dance.

Four waiting to relieve any kitten that might get tired and freak dance.

Toward the center of the awning, three booty-dancing kittens hold up a boom box, which steadily pumps out techno music. Three more stand in the wings to relieve them if they get tired, and while they wait, they also booty dance.

Cody picked the awning that best suited him. A ten-foot-tall print of a yellow kitten silhouetted against a bright orange background. The orange because it complements his kittens, which are mostly tabbies. The yellow because it complements his red raincoat. The kitten stands for his fiery vengeance.

Initially, it was just him and his kittens. Now there is also a large group of people, which grows larger the further he goes up Blue Street. Apparently, it's people trying to come out from the debris and youngsters coming out to 'freak it' with his kittens, possibly with hopes of getting on television. According to many of the youths coming in, he is 'it,' and the 'party is on' under Cody's awning (which has now been dubbed 'the party awning') as it bounces up Blue Street.

Cody doesn't mind all the company. His kittens are happy, and more people means more help with carrying the awning. This is good. He would be on time. Maybe the mob will cheer him on when he shoots his sister. That will also be nice.

***

Shelly, Teddy, Boss, and Kenny stand in front of Blue Street's historic sculpture. The sculpture, named The Duke after the sculptor who sculpted it, could very easily pass for a garden-variety twenty-foot-tall revolver. They've stopped because the statue is one of the principle works of art by the most major artist of the Cowboy Movement.

Shelly's not bothered by the fact Kenny and Boss need to stop in front of the statue. Cowboys had been making pilgrimages to see The Duke ever since it was erected. Today, as always, there is a large group of cowboys—all with Stetson hats, leather chaps, six-shooters, and mustaches of varying lengths and thickness—gathered in front of the statue. Some interested cowboys overhear Kenny, who has been drinking steadily since they left the bridge, as he launches into a drunken rant concerning the meaning of The Duke and what he says is "its justification as an artistic marvel in the contemporary world." Intrigued, they begin to drift over.

"This here statue," he slurs in his cowboy drawl, "not only immortalizes the traditional cowboy weapon, but also the way it's been put up against the backdrop of that there Rainbow City skyline. It juxtaposes folks' modern ideas of urbanality against more historicized ideas of growth and progress."

The group of cowboys closest to Kenny all nod their Stetson-hatted heads and mutter their agreement. Kenny smoothes out his mustache in approval. Shelly rolls her eyes and wonders if they wouldn't have been better off staying on the bridge and shooting puppies. Indeed, the statue is pretty. The metal is the bluest of cobalt blues, which contrasts nicely against the sky, and the cherry wood stock is bursting with such complex character Shelly sometimes thinks she could get lost in it for days. But it was not, as Kenny points out, "What we honest folk like to think of as an anti-meta-social-commentary."

Thankfully, they're not too far away from the Town Hall. Shelly can see it just up Blue Street, and the large clock out front tells her she still has some time. This is good. There's no telling when she'll be able to pull Kenny away from The Duke, especially now that he has an audience and can explain to them the subtle intricacies of color choice.

Shelly hears techno music, looks back down Blue Street, and sees a large crowd of people coming up.

They're a bit far off, but Shelly can tell that the group's comprised of an awning, people, and kittens. And all of them appear to be embraced in some kind of hedonistic orgy. A voice breaks her concentration.

"Excuse me, partner." A striking cowboy separates himself from those standing around The Duke and walks toward Kenny. Shelly's breath catches in her throat, and she falls to the ground as her knees buckle. The cowboy before them stands a head taller than any other cowboy. His face is as rugged as his cowboy clothing. Of all the cowboys that Shelly has known, his mustache is easily the fullest and richest. He is the most rugged, most handsome, most 'cowboy' cowboy Shelly has ever seen. Other cowboys around him look more so like cowboys because of him. He is Cowboy Rick. Never in her life had Shelly thought she had the remotest chance of meeting him in person.

"What can I do for you, partner?" Cowboy Kenny eyes Cowboy Rick. Cowboy Rick eyes Cowboy Kenny. They search each other for signs of any hint of cowboy inferiority and find nothing. Mutual respect forms instantaneously.

"You seem to have an eye for art. What's your name, son?"

"It's a gift," Kenny's face, already red from Moldy Poison, blushes redder at the compliment, "and you can call me Kenny."

"Well, Kenny, my name's Rick. I noticed that you seem to know your art and that you got a knack for speakin'. You ever consider a career in television?"

Shelly's knees are jelly. Teddy does his best to hold her up as she hyperventilates. Boss drinks from the bottle, and Kenny is at a loss for words. They all now notice the television crew. Several men and women stand behind Cowboy Rick with cameras and boom microphones. The lone producer stands with a headset on her head and a clipboard in hand. She whispers into her headset and then holds her breath, waiting to see what will happen.

"I thought *Cowboys* was cancelled," says Boss, the first of the group to find their voice. "How you gonna put Kenny on TV when you ain't got no show?"

Cowboy Rick smiles wide as a rainbow at the mention of the reality TV show. "*Cowboys* is cancelled because the network thought they'd get better ratings if they gave me my own show," he pauses, then continues, "The Cowboy Rick Show."

Shelly can't believe what she's hearing. She shouts, "Oh my God! I love you, Rick!"

Cowboy Rick looks warmly over to Shelly and says, "Why, aren't you a pretty little thing?" Shelly nearly faints.

"They're giving you your own show?" asks Kenny.

"Actually, that's why I'm here," says Cowboy Rick, jutting his thumb in the direction of the statue. "I'm fixin' to do a piece on The Duke."

This is the best day of Shelly's life. Cowboy Rick's getting his own show, and he just called her pretty. She is so overwhelmed she can barely move. Teddy sits her down, takes her glass, fills it, and hands it to her. Cowboy Kenny shakes Cowboy Rick's hand, and they begin discussing how Kenny might approach the topic of The Duke for Rick's show.

Shelly hears her heart beating inside of her chest. Cowboy Rick asks Cowboy Kenny if he and his friends want to go out for coffee with his producer, and Kenny says yes. The film crew is constantly angling for better shots. She can hear her heart beating louder and begins to think it might be beating too loudly when she realizes it's not her heart she's hearing, it's techno music accompanied by the faint sound of coughing.

The air is filled with the sight of smoke and the sound of gunshots.

***

Certain he's caught a glimpse of his green and red striped umbrella in the crowd of cowboys surrounding The Duke, Cody calls for the party awning to halt. Nothing happens. He walks over to the stereo, turns down the music and they stop. The kittens and party awning-ers eye him questioningly. He takes his gun out of his pocket.

"I'm doing this for you," he says, knowing that his sister must die if there is any chance of them maintaining their happiness. Since he had left the apartment, every once-in-a-while a part of him would wonder if he was capable of shooting his twin sister. They were blood, after all. But then another part of him, the part that loves kittens and joy, would insist that his sister had to die. The truth was he simply had more love for the things that loved him back. He couldn't remember the last time his sister showed him any emotion that wasn't drunken annoyance. His kittens exuded love. All he had to do was look into their eyes, and he could see it. When it came down to deciding importance, he owed his sister nothing and his kittens everything. And in this case, he owed them his sister's life.

He tries to find his umbrella in the crowd, but it's gone, lost in a sea of cowboys. It'd be impossible to navigate the crowd, so Cody does the next best thing.

He makes sure each end of the awning is being held firmly by his kittens, and gets some other folks to boost him up atop the awning. Once on top, he addresses the crowd.

"Alright, everybody, listen up!" yells Cody, taking out his pistol and firing up into the air.

The whole crowd of cowboys looks up, sees a boy standing atop an awning holding a pistol, and begins to cheer all at once. This is not the desired effect. Cody fires again. The cheering gets louder and all the cowboys, following Cody's lead, take out their pistols and fire them into the air. Hundreds of bullets race upward. Gun smoke fills the streets and visibility is reduced to zero.

"Shelly!" shouts Cody and he waits for the smoke to clear.

He hears someone yelling, "Cody!" But the voice is faint.

"Cody!" It's closer this time, and the second Cody sees his sister run out of the crowd towards him. She stops a few feet away when he levels his pistol at her.

"Cody, what are you doing?" Standing in her raincoat, Shelly eyes her brother's pistol and takes a drink.

Cody tries to think of an answer to his sister's question. He can't think of one. Not one that she would understand, anyway. Understanding required empathy, and there was no way that his sister would ever be able to understand anything that didn't directly relate to her. She was too selfish. How do you explain a personal vendetta to a selfish person?

Finally, he says, "You deserve this, Shelly," as he begins to squeeze the trigger.

***

Even with a gun pointed at her, Shelly has never felt better in her life.

"Cody," she says, "you look upset." She looks down the barrel of her brother's gun and wonders what could have possibly gotten him into such a tizzy.

A look of confusion comes across Cody's face, and his trigger finger drops down to the gun's grip.

"Since when have you ever cared if I look upset?" he asks pointedly.

Teddy appears behind Shelly, umbrella held firmly in one fuzzy hand. Cody still stares confusedly at his sister, gun shaking in his hand. Shelly begins to speak again, but Cody interrupts her.

"You're going to kill me by taking away everything good in my life, and I'm going to kill you before I let that happen."

Shelly looks at Cody holding his shaking gun, then at the group of people and inbred kittens under the party awning. They're all gently bouncing to the soft techno beat coming from the turned-down stereo. They look like they're coiling their bodies so that they can be ready to leap into action as soon as the music is turned back up. Every few moments, a kitten stares longingly at the stereo and then Shelly gets it. She understands.

Cody loves booty dancing as much as she loves cowboys. No wonder he's so mad. She turns back to her brother.

"This is about that note I left on the table this morning about trying to get booty dancing banned, isn't it?"

Cody nods his head. He looks tentative, as if she has just said the last thing he would have expected to hear from his sister. He drops his gun, jumps down from the awning, and runs toward his sister.

Shelly wants to say that she was sorry, and that she no longer has any intention of trying to get booty dancing banned. But she is only able to say "Well, I guess I'm sorry tha….." before Cody embraces her with the full force of a bear hug, and all her air is forced out of her lungs.

Cheers roar from the party awning. The kittens turn up the stereo. The cowboys whoop and holler and, again, fire their guns in the air.

"You know," says Shelly to her brother after some time has passed. "Cowboy Rick asked a bunch of us out for coffee. I think I'm going to do that instead of the Town Hall meeting. Did you want to come with us?"

"Um," Cody motions to the crowd under his awning. "I got all these folks with me." The dancing is now more furious than ever.

"You could just leave them outside for a bit. I don't think they'll hurt anything."

"Well…" Cody thinks for a moment. She has a point. If, as they said, the party was always "on" under the party awning, then it would still be "on" after they got back from coffee.

"Okay," he says.

***

Shelly, Teddy, Cody, and Cowboys Rick, Kenny, and Boss all sit down at an outside table and order coffee. The camera crew stands back at a respectable distance.

"It sure makes me happy that you two were able to work out your differences," says Cowboy Kenny to the two siblings. "I think it's a shame when a brother and sister can't get along."

"Yup," says Boss, "you two just need to remember to keep the lines of communication open."

"I'd say," says Cowboy Rick. "It's been my experience that the only result we can expect from ignoring problems is more problems."

The camera crew pans in for a single shot of Rick to fully capture his sage advice.

"I agree," says Teddy. "No good ever comes from ignoring your problems."

The bear uncorks the bottle of whiskey and tops off his and Shelly's coffee. Cody coughs violently several times. Everyone agrees that today is a good day. Up Blue Street, the Town Hall explodes.

Kayfabe

Steve is smashing my head into concrete outside the ring. It's not as bad as it looks, but I try to make it look as bad as possible. I should be performing better, and my marriage problems are to blame.

Steve doesn't like me, and I don't like him. If you don't like someone, you fight them. It's the quickest, easiest, and most satisfying course to conflict resolution.

Usually, your head gets slammed against things when you fight. My head's always been a popular target and, right now, a large mass of scar tissue on it has broken open and begun to bleed. Both Steve and I are happy about the blood because it makes the fight look good, and that's essential to what we do.

The reason I don't like Steve: his friend, Hank, shattered my friend Jimmy's knee with a lead pipe.

At the time, I had tried to save my friend Jimmy by running down a long dimly-lit hallway to his rescue. I was thwarted when Steve jumped out from behind a corner and hit me over the head with a metal folding chair. And so as I lay, concussed, really concussed, on the floor, Hank brought down the full force of his hatred, in the form of a lead pipe, on my good friend Jimmy's knee. Cameras caught the whole thing, and the lighting was perfect. The audience at the Wings Stadium arena was absolutely shocked. Many trucker hats were sold.

I have reason not to like Steve. I've reason not to like the way he conducts himself, and this angle means we get in the ring and fight most nights for the foreseeable future. My cause is just, and it's right that I should win. Steve is now the hated one.

Steve and I are actually very good friends. My dislike for him is kayfabe. Jimmy's shattered knee is also kayfabe. Hank did give it a good whack with a pipe, though it wasn't a real lead pipe. Lead pipes aren't around anymore because no one wants to drink water with lead in it. It was decided that Hank's aluminum pipe would be a kayfabe lead pipe because it sounded more tough and fit Hank's gimmick and sold more merchandise. We sell 'Hank's Lead Pipe' to children, but it is made of Styrofoam because parents don't want their kids whacking each other with heavy metal.

Hank's gimmick: he's a union plumber. His name: Hank the Union Plumber.

Jimmy is my kayfabe friend and also my actual friend, or at least he thinks he is. I don't really consider him my friend, which means he's not. I don't like Jimmy much because he flirted with my wife last year at a Christmas party when he thought no one was looking. He also flirted with her at the New Year's party when he thought no one was looking, and at a meet-and-greet two years ago. He was wrong to think he was any kind of sly because I saw him every time.

My wife no longer wishes to see me, but I'd still like to fight Jimmy. I would like to meet him on the street and slam his head into a concrete sidewalk in a way that hurt as bad as it looked. I've spent many nights in hotel rooms thinking about the various ways I could make Jimmy wish he hadn't hit on my wife, but I cannot do these things, because fights that aren't kayfabe and in rings get you arrested and don't sell merchandise.

Twenty thousand people chant my name as Steve stops driving my head into the mat with his large black boot, stands me up, and punches me a few times in the solar plexus. This doesn't hurt as much as I make it look.

At some point, I'll beat up Steve. At some point, one of us will win, but I can't remember who or how, and this is going to be a problem. I'm a bit confused today. My head's still kind of concussed and fuzzy from last night when Steve accidently dropped me on my head. The mat smells like stale sweat and alcohol wipes. Steve picks me up and lifts me over his head and throws me back down. Twenty thousand people want me to kick Steve's ass and chant the name that is printed in red brick letters across the back of my tight black shorts.

"Solid Mike!" they yell.

The 'I' in 'Solid' and 'Mike' is represented with yellow lightning bolts. I don't feel the crowd's enthusiasm like I normally do. My wife has left me. The crowd knows this.

Solid Mike's my fighting name. I used to have a different name but I had to change it years ago because I lost a namefight to a man with the same name as me. Our name: The Patriot. We didn't like each other because we felt the other was not patriotic enough, and so we got into the ring and fought over who got to keep it. Now my name's Solid Mike. That's 'Solid Mike,' in red brick letters with two lightning bolts.

The name on my birth certificate, my Florida marriage license, and on the title to my house is Howard Finkle. My parents named me Howard after Howard Hughes, the great American entrepreneur and are very proud of my accomplishments. Wait, that's not right. My parents named me Howard after Howard Namerov, the great American poet. I'm pretty sure they actually hated Howard Hughes.

I sign into hotels under the name Jacob Johnson because most of my fans know the name Howard Finkle and bother me if they find I'm staying in a hotel that is within driving distance of their homes.

When my two daughters in Florida talk about me to other people, they use the name Solid Mike, and so does my wife. They do this so people will know who I am. Sometimes older people do not recognize the name Solid Mike, and when this happens, they mention I used to be The Patriot.

My wife and kids spend the majority of their time in Tampa, Florida. The kids, who my wife no longer wishes me to see, are very active in school and extracurriculars. The youngest takes jujitsu lessons and plays the bassoon. The oldest runs track and is president of the debate team.

They're both at an age where neither of them thinks it's very cool to be the child of Solid Mike. When they're happy with me, they call me Dad. When they're not, they call me Solid Mike in a way that makes me feel very small. I miss them both dearly.

Kayfabe

My wife, who currently serves as a Florida State Senator, attends various community and social events where she gets hit on. This is because many people, like Jimmy, are attracted to the fact she's a skinny waif of a thing with small but plump breasts, curly red hair, and a face that stops traffic. All of this is very helpful to her political career, and she's currently in a rather heated race for a seat on the United States House of Representatives. Probably she will win; political analysts say she has just the right combination of confident intelligence and elegant beauty.

My kayfabe wife has enormous fake breasts, bleach blonde hair, and a nose that is too small for her face. Her name is Nexus. Currently Nexus isn't happy with me, and we've been having a lot of arguments in rooms that are lit in ways that show the full brunt of our emotional toil. But I still love her dearly, and this is all that matters.

Steve mocks my marriage after he lifts me up over his shoulder and slams me down. The crowd screams for me to get it together. Steve's words are unkind. He says my kayfabe wife's reputation for promiscuity is well-known.

"Nexus is a hoe," he says, grinding his knee in my face.

Nexus and I fell in love years ago when we met at a fundraiser for multiple sclerosis. Wait, that's not right. That's where I met and fell in love with my actual wife.

Nexus and I fell in love when one of my matches was interrupted by Steve and Hank. They ran into the ring and rendered me unconscious by concussing my brain with their pipes and metal folding chairs. I was saved when Nexus ran to the ring and frenziedly struck Steve and Hank with her metal folding chair, knocking them out and giving them concussions.

All of this was kayfabe except for the concussions. There are many concussions in my business and few of them are kayfabe because kayfabe injuries must be visible for us to have any chance of selling them.

The name on Nexus's birth certificate is Jennifer Holt. This name is also on her California marriage license, along with her wife's name. Jennifer's wife's is almost as attractive as my own. I've met her, she seems very nice.

"You broke Jimmy's knee," I say to Steve, blood dripping from my forehead down my face. Jimmy's full fighting name is Jimmy Jamm. The fans love his smile, and this sells lots of merchandise.

"Hank did," corrects Steve, "Hank broke Jimmy's knee, and he deserved it!" He's right. It was Hank who busted Jimmy's knee with a lead pipe, not Steve. This all gets very confusing sometimes.

Steve gets me to my feet and swings my body, head first, into one of the four metal poles supporting the ring. This further tears open the mass of scar tissue on my forehead. Also, it probably worsens a concussion I got in Charlotte yesterday when Steve accidently dropped me directly on my head. There's enough blood now that the smell should be clearly pungent for the screaming audience members standing in the front rows. This is a treat for them. They wear my lightning bolt t-shirts and love the sight of my blood.

"Don't you say nothin' bad about Janet!" I say, wiping my eyes.

"Nexus," corrects Steve, "Nexus is a hoe."

Kayfabe

"Don't you say nothin' bad 'bout her, either!" I yell back, louder this time. I've been breaking kayfabe a lot lately and it's bad, completely unprofessional.

Steve and I've fought many times. Our current match is particularly important, only I can't remember why. This gets confusing sometimes. Guess it could be the concussions, but part of this is Creative's fault. Creative has taken complete control of my angles because they think my ideas are no longer complex enough for our audience.

Creative has also taken control of Steve's angles and, like me, he's pretty pissed about it.

Steve's full fighting name: Long-Haul Steve. He also lives in Tampa, Florida. The name on the title of his house: Franklin Palmer. The occupation listed on his tax return: Professional Sports Entertainer.

His kayfabe occupation, his gimmick: he's a truck driver. He comes to the ring in a green flannel shirt and blue trucker hat and has joined up with Hank the Plumber to start The Union of Devastation. When they tagteam, their finishing move is Union Local 187. Steve's finishing move is called The Truck Driver. Currently, they're both actively recruiting other fighters into their kayfabe union. Even holding kayfabe union elections where the fans get to vote on representatives. Merchandise is flying off the shelves.

"You're no kind of man anymore," says Steve, "no kind of father." The crowd's screaming at me to get up.

He's right about Nexus. We are fighting, and I'm a questionable father. The twins are kayfabe. I got Nexus kayfabe pregnant, and she wore a prosthetic tummy for three months and wrestled in a magenta floral print maternity dress and sold a lot of merchandise.

A nice set was created for our house. Cameras were placed in ideal positions, and lights were set up to capture the emotion in Nexus's face as she sang to her belly and suffered strange food cravings and got emotional over dramatic television programming. We had many televised moments during her pregnancy. It was decided I should turn heel, go bad, and I had to strike her in order to get my fans to turn against me. This worked like a charm. Very few people want to cheer for an abusive husband. Simple as that. If you want the audience to dislike you, hit a woman, or better still, you hit your pregnant wife.

This was when I had to change my name from The Patriot to Solid Mike. The other Patriot said striking women wasn't very American. I played heel for one year and developed a kayfabe drinking problem and refused to fight fair until one night when Nexus got into some trouble. I swooped in with a baseball bat and saved her, and she forgave me, which effectively ended my heelness. Fans still talk about this dark period in my life.

There are many rules in this business, the number one rule: never break kayfabe. Keeping kayfabe is necessary for maintaining the audience's suspension of disbelief. Two nights ago, while fighting Steve, I stated that Jimmy couldn't fight because of his strained neck which, of course, is wrong.

The kayfabe reason Jimmy cannot fight is because his knee was shattered by Hank's lead pipe. The reason stated on Jimmy's website, and Wikipedia, and on many fan blogs is he suffers from a severe neck muscle strain and must let it mend before performing again.

Kayfabe

The real reason: Jimmy's in rehab, kicking a prescription pill addiction. Few people know this. Management decided it was time to send Jimmy to rehab when he got too belligerent at a company dinner and hit on the owner's wife when he thought no one was looking.

Creative went to work, and a few nights later, Hank shattered Jimmy's knee with a lead pipe in a hallway which was lit in a way the cameras could perfectly capture the hatred on Hank's face as he brought down the pipe. Yeah, the angle's good because now every night at least twenty thousand people cheer for me, hold up signs proclaiming my vengeance of Jimmy's attack and buy my merchandise. With Jimmy out, more fans spend their money on my stuff. But it's not because Creative's coming up with good ideas; they just got lucky because Jimmy's a no-good dope head who can't keep his dick in his pants.

Steve climbs up to the top rope, jumps off, and lands on my chest, elbow-first. A sharp thud sound emanates out from the ring and reaches out to the edges of Wings Stadium arena. I make this look like it hurts worse than it does. Though, I'm not sure my grimace is grimace-y enough. The crowd screams my name. I've no idea how this match ends. This is a problem.

I haven't been performing great lately. I get confused sometimes. The doctor says it's due to an accumulation of concussions. Thankfully, the audience isn't expecting my best effort because my mind isn't completely on the match. They know I'm distracted by my marriage problems.

Weeks ago, a set was created for my wife Nexus and I to have an argument. Lights were set up so that the emotion on our faces could be clearly lit and accented as we passionately screamed at each other. She was mad because I forgot her birthday; she was mad because I forgot our anniversary. She said I was never around and neglected our children. That I was obsessed with my feud with Steve and she was leaving me, so I struck her, and the cameras caught everything. We sold a hell of a lot of merchandise.

Wait, that's not right.

My actual wife was mad about these things. She was mad because I forgot her birthday and anniversary. She said I was never around and was neglecting our children. She said that she wanted to separate and for me to leave and not to come back, so I struck her. I struck my actual wife.

I don't think there were any cameras there.

Come to think of it, I don't think there was any special attempt to light our faces as that usually only happens with Nexus.

Steve kicks me in the head. This doesn't hurt so bad, but he puts too much on it, and my brain gets jarred, and the air's filled with the smell of overripe fruit.

"You're weak," he says. "That's why Nexus is going to leave you."

Steve throws me against the ropes, I dodge his clothesline, bounce off the opposite ropes and clothesline him. Screams of joy rip though the audience, and it's so loud I can feel their roar in my bones.

Nexus has been doing well for quite a while, but we aren't getting along anymore, though I still love her. Two weeks ago, she told me she was leaving me for Hank the

Kayfabe

Plumber. She said she's part of The Union, that she's running for union representative.

She said she was leaving and taking our children and then hit me over the head with a metal folding chair. All this was done on the set of our brightly-lit kayfabe home. Everyone thinks this is tragic, especially considering my current feud with Steve.

No one knows I struck my actual wife. No one knows we're separated.

My wife says no one wants to vote for a woman whose husband beats her, so she's keeping everything quiet. She says that if I have any respect left for her or our children, I'll keep it quiet, too. She says she doesn't want me around anymore because she's afraid of what I might do.

I drive my elbow into Steve's chest and wish I knew how this was suppose to end.

"You're pathetic!" bellows Steve. He spits and then adds, "Your wife doesn't want you."

"I still love my wife!" I reply, and pick Steve up over my head and slam him down on the mat. He lies motionless on the ground as I get out of the ring and get a metal folding chair.

My notoriety got my wife elected to State Senate, and now it's going to get her elected to the National House of Representatives. My yearly earning potential is seven figures, and she doesn't want me to see our kids.

Steve's getting up when I climb back into the ring and whack his head. Probably this gives him a concussion. I don't much care; it's part of the business.

One of the ringside announcers pounds his fist on the announcing table and then proceeds to scratch his nose. This means the match is over in ninety seconds. This is not good.

I don't remember how this is supposed to end.

Steve gets up, and I hit him again. A cut opens up on his face, and fans can probably smell the blood fifteen rows up. This is good. We're going to sell a lot of merchandise.

The crowd screams as Nexus runs into the arena and down the aisle with a metal folding chair. She's wearing a blue pin-striped pantsuit with a yellow button attached to the lapel that reads VOTE FOR NEXUS.

"I don't want to see you anymore," she says, and my kayfabe wife baseball-swings the chair toward my head.

"This marriage is over!" she yells and prepares another swing. "You're never going to see your children again!"

I fall to my knees. I remember how this match ends.

White Fields and Emerson

It seems to me all the smart life took a cue from evolution and beat feet south or decided to take a four-month nap. Not us humans, though. Our brains have made us stupid, and the cold makes us more so. Every winter, I feel a primal urge to migrate south, and when I fail to do this, my body does its best to hibernate and wishes for a dinosaur.

A dinosaur or transcendence.

So, I'm in a frozen field of gray and white trying to transcend. Emerson says, "It is the quality of the moment, not the number of days, or events, or of actors, that imports." I take this to mean that I should try to be happy even though I believe that the only animal capable of happiness during a Wisconsin winter is the penguin, and we don't have penguins in Wisconsin, and I'm not a penguin. Although, when I was young, I wanted to be a dinosaur. I'm sorry, that was a lie. I still want to be a dinosaur. Even with the small arms and hands of a Tyrannosaurus rex, the winter would be far more tolerable. Sure, there would be some difficulty in throwing snowballs, but really, who is going to start a snowball fight with a T-rex? Even if someone did, it would make this colorless field more interesting when I ate them.

The snow is as white as white, and the wind is cold. It's February, the northern quarter of the United States has been without enough sun for too long and so have I. Everything has taken on its own particular shade of gray. This is partially because snow has covered the brown grass and evergreens and partially because the salt has drifted from the roads to cover everything else.

Perhaps some sort of image would help, like maybe a red image probably would help. It might make this field somewhat more manageable. Red and white go together, don't they? I forget what red looks like. The dinosaurs never had this problem, and I'm jealous because the earth was warm still when they walked around in their tropical Pangaea.

There is an intense reflection from the sun off of the snow, but this, of course, does not add any color. The sun's too far away from the earth, and its light is different. It's a gray quality, a compact florescent light bulb quality, bright and ugly and not quite the right quality. Not the most ideal of combinations because one always accentuates the others (the bright makes the ugly uglier and the ugly makes the gray grayer, and this all goes a long way to making everything look as though it would look better if it looked some other way), which causes an ever worsening cycle of the three elements getting stronger and then feeding back into each other until all observers have soaked in so much gray that they can't even recognize it anymore. It's inside them now. Internalized. They think that this is the way it has always been. This is the way the earth looks. This is all the natural color I have ever known. I have no reason to expect otherwise. Brilliance is a fantasy, and the dinosaurs are dead.

A car, a dusty black car, drives past the street behind me and a rusty tracker behind it.

The air is dry and cold and smells like restaurant grease and car exhaust and the only sound comes from wind and passing cars thumping their bass. There is no life and no color, nope, only people gorging themselves on Burger King as they move from place to place on gray roads in cars shaded the same, and I try to imagine non-gray.

My bones feel tired. Apparently, my body feels it must conserve energy for times when I can wake up to the sound of playing squirrels and singing birds and smell fresh-cut grass as I watch bumblebees gather pollen from blooming flowers that I distinctly remember as having a color different from the one color I see now.

I make an effort to count the number of things I can see that are gray. I stop when I reach number one and decide to try and imagine what the same field looks like in the summer. I conjure a beach ball in the center of the empty field resting gently atop the snow. Probably, the beach ball is an improvement, so I leave it there and wonder if what I've done is transcendental.

Maybe, I think. I think maybe I've put a beach ball in this field because I wished to live deliberately, to front only the essential facts of life, and see if I could not learn what it had to teach, and not, when I came to die, discover that I had not lived.

Having worked this out, I move the beach ball two feet to the left of its previous spot and change it from a beach ball to a dinosaur—specifically, a Tyrannosaurus rex. I name him Rex. A transcendental name.

Rex turns his scaly head to me and begins to speak: "A single footstep will not make a path on the earth, so a single thought will not make a pathway in the mind. To make a deep physical path, we walk again and again. To make a deep mental path, we must think over and over the kind of thoughts we wish to dominate our lives."

Rex is right.

I give him a nice big recliner, bifocals, a smoking jacket, a fireplace, a bookcase, and a beach ball.

"You're a T-rex," I point out. "A single one of your footsteps would make a path for me."

He puts on his jacket.

"Your argument then," I continue, "is inconsistent."

Rex sits down in his chair next to the fireplace, takes a book off the shelf, and affixes his bifocals.

"A foolish consistency," he says, once he has found the correct page, "is the hobgoblin of Tyrannosaurus-rexes."

He stands for a moment, then lumbers over to the wood bin, where he picks up a cedar log with one of his tiny arms and throws it on the fire. I'm impressed at his accuracy, considering how uselessly tiny his arms are.

"Good throw," I say.

White Fields and Emerson

"Thoreau?" he asks, then says, "No," pointing to his book, "that was Emerson."

I pause for a moment.

"I don't think that's right," I say.

The cedar log is burning, and the field is filled with a pleasant aroma.

"You look tired," says Rex, as he motions to another (much smaller) recliner across from his on the other side of the fireplace. "Why don't you sit down and relax for a little bit?"

"Thanks," I say. "I've just been really stressed out lately. I've never been very good with winters."

"A dinosaur is what he thinks about all day long," says Rex, adjusting his bifocals as he reads from his book.

"I don't think that's right," I say.

It's interesting. People never missed dinosaurs until they realized that they were gone and they weren't coming back. At least spring is coming back. At least color was coming back. At least I have a quiet moment to share with Rex in this field next to the sweet smell of burning cedar.

This seems much better than sitting at a fast food restaurant.

I look up at Rex. "You probably think our fast food places are absurd, don't you?"

Rex, whose tiny hand is now holding a Whopper, shakes his head. "These Whoppers are fucking great," he says and then throws the burger up in the air and catches it in his mouth.

"Nice throw," I say.

"I don't think that's right," he says and tosses me a Whopper.

"So, what do you think of the winter?" I ask, knowing full well that Rex had never had winter because he lived 200 million years ago during the Jurassic period when the climate was much hotter than it is now.

"The fire's nice," says Rex, as he somewhat difficultly tries to maneuver the book in his tiny arms to a place where one of the eyes on the side of his head can see it.

"But, what about all the cold and gray?"

"Well, nature always wears the colors of the spirit. Nature and books belong to the eyes that see them." The dinosaur stops for a moment to page through his book. "Also, nature hates calculators."

And the field is empty again. Perhaps Rex is right. Perhaps all I need to avoid seeing the gray is to look at things differently. Maybe rusty cars and salty roads can be as brilliant as a rainbow in the spring. And, actually, that grease smells pretty good. Maybe that dinosaur had the right idea. Maybe I should be a Whopper.

I know that Rex might say that Whoppers are only good food for dinosaurs.

But I don't think that's right.

Reptiles in Tijuana

Stewart called his wife, Janet, from his car on the way home from work.

"Did he come?"

"Yes, Stewie, he came."

"Is he beautiful?"

"Yes, Stewie, you know he is."

Once inside his apartment, Stewart saw the crocodile's tail jutting out from the study. He quickly stepped over the tail so he could get into the doorway and see his new acquisition in all its reptilian glory.

Janet was sitting at the desk, and his new crocodile lay next to her in its pool of dark murky water. The crocodile was so remarkable that he could barely handle his emotions, and for a moment, he felt tears swell.

Its scales were as big as Stewart's eyes, and they were the color and texture of stone. It was at least three feet wide and had ridge after ridge of bone plate starting from its head all the way back to the tip of its tail. There were no muscles in its face and yet it still looked like it was smiling about some secret.

Stewart had just gotten a promotion, and with that promotion came a new office, new responsibilities, respect within the company, and enough money to buy a crocodile. This was Stewart's new crocodile.

The reptile lay perfectly motionless, not even its eyes moved, yet it seemed to be watching those in the room the same way that eyes in art portraits appear to follow those nearby. Stewart's ecstasy presented itself as a warm buzz that started at the base of his skull and spread quickly throughout the rest of his body.

"What do you think of Kyle?" he asked Janet, who was sitting at the desk browsing some nature website just a few feet away from the crocodile and its pool of muddy saltwater.

Janet turned to him, "You know, I have never felt more comfortable," she paused thoughtfully, "in my life. Kyle really knows how to make a girl feel safe." She motioned toward the crocodile, and the gigantic reptile picked up its enormous head and moved slightly to the left before settling back into the mud. "Just look at him. You can already tell he's protective of me." Kyle's massive jaws were completely submerged in dark water, but its eyes were still visible. "I feel like I've been so much more productive ever since they dropped him off."

Stewart studied Kyle proudly. The reptilian eye that looked at him winked twice with two sets of eyelids, one vertical and one horizontal. Stewart winked back as he was certain their friendship had begun.

"Has he eaten yet?" he asked, and then noticed the pig sitting in the opposite corner of the room.

"I don't really understand it," said Janet, "but Kyle doesn't seem interested. Ever since they brought Kyle and Porky in, all they do is stare at each other."

The pig had to be at least two hundred pounds and was as round as a barrel. It looked everything like a pig: pink, fat, and piggish right down to the spiral tail. It sat on a small pile of hay beneath the window with its eyes fixed on the giant croc. Every once in a while, the pig oinked.

Stewart figured Kyle would eventually get hungry, though he wasn't sure he liked the idea of Janet getting so familiar with their crocodile's meals.

"You shouldn't have named the pig," he said. "It's not good to get attached."

"Hey," said Janet, turning her head back to the computer screen, "I like Porky. He's got personality."

Stewart eyed the pig in an attempt to discover the personality to which his wife was referring. The pig stared blankly at Stewart. It oinked.

"But it's food."

"Whatever," said Janet. For a second, her smile reminded him of Kyle's, like she knew something he didn't. "If it happens, it happens. It's the circle of life."

Stewart wrinkled his nose in disapproval and walked out of the office, going down the hallway into the kitchen. The discussion about food had made him hungry. "Did you pick up ice cream today?" He shouted at the open doorway with the giant ridged tail protruding from it.

"I didn't have time, and the caterers will be here soon. Why don't you walk down to the store and let me worry about the party."

Not really wanting to deal with the caterers, Stewart left happily. As he walked down the street, the sun shined upon his face and glinted off the window of La Che Le Rue. Now that he had Kyle, he might even be able to get a table there. Before today, such a thing would have been impossible.

At the corner store, he picked up the ice cream because Janet was always forgetting to buy him his Rocky Road.

***

"What a wonderful alligator," remarked the wife of a VP, while sipping her merlot.

The caterers had made certain the apartment was finely appointed. They had even gone so far as to place a drink waiter directly in front of Kyle, and a waiter with hors d'oeuvres in front of Porky.

"It's not an alligator, it's a crocodile," Stewart corrected her. "Saltwater, Crocodylus porosus, from Indonesia."

"One of the biggest crocodiles I've ever seen," commented the director of technical operations, while he sipped his gin martini.

"He's actually the biggest on record," Stewart corrected, smiling and sipping a vodka martini.

"What's the pig doing here?" asked Ted's wife, Marge.

The pig seemed to notice that it was being talked about, and greeted her with a look of mild disinterest. She stared back in kind. The pig oinked.

"Porky should eventually be Kyle's first meal," answered Janet, holding her cosmopolitan away from her body and shifting her hips toward the crocodile. "But I'm starting to think they like each other."

Stewarts's boss, Ted, was pleasantly impressed with the croc. "That's one beautiful animal you got there, Stewart. He's going to be a big hit."

Stewart thanked him again, and Ted laughed warmly. "Do you like golf?"

Drinks were poured. The night went long. The majority of Kyle's head lay unmoving in its pool with only its eyes above the water, while the heads of the company oohed and aahed. Every once in a while, Kyle blinked its two sets of eyelids in succession and the oohs and aahs would begin anew.

At the end of the night, Stewart and Janet found themselves alone with Stewart's boss, Ted, and his drunken wife, Marge.

"I heard the VP of technology just got himself a Galápagos tortoise," said Marge. The waiter again took away her empty glass and replaced it with a full one.

"Goddamn show-off," commented Ted under his breath as he sipped his fresh martini.

"Harvey, from accounts receivable, they say he just picked up his second Komodo dragon."

"Oh, my god," Janet chuckled. "Could you get any more cliché?"

"Well," said Marge, "I can tell you that that saltwater croc you've picked out is a good one." Marge paused for a moment. "What's his name? Lyle?"

"Kyle," said Stewart. "His name is Kyle."

"Kyle?" asked Marge.

Ted had several poison dart frogs and a Colorado River Toad. Marge was always mentioning how poison dart frogs were nearly extinct; also, that the Colorado River toad could be licked for a high that was like no other. She'd given the frogs all names of past presidents.

Problem was that everybody knew that Ted didn't really care for frogs, didn't even like to lick them. What was the point of having a Colorado River toad if you didn't even lick it?

"You've got a fine animal there, Stewart," said Ted, looking at Kyle, "a fine animal. You know, I wasn't kidding about that golf game."

***

Stewart had to admit that being the head of the division was certainly better than being a part of it. He felt he was a better person now that he had his own crocodile. He no longer felt drained by the never ending columns of numbers it was his job to keep in order. Recently, his work had seemed much easier, and life was good.

That morning, his wife had told him she wanted to take Kyle out and show it off to some of Marge's lunch friends. It had only been a couple of weeks, and they had already made sufficient advances up the social strata. Soon, the three of them would be unstoppable.

However, Stewart was beginning to be bothered by the pig. It had been almost two weeks, and Kyle still hadn't eaten it.

"I'm going to leave the office door open and let Porky go where he likes," Janet had announced that morning. She had her hands on her hips in a way that meant there would be little room for argument.

Stewart had tried to be staunch, saying, "Janet, he's food."

Janet was stauncher. "I don't think Kyle's going to eat him. Look at them, they're friends."

"But..." Stewart marched into the study and observed the two animals. They were staring at each other. When they noticed him, they broke their eye contact. There were no signs of a predator-prey relationship. Janet was right, and although this wasn't something that normally bothered him, it was one of the first times in recent memory that Stewart was happy to leave for work.

"How are you settling in, Stewart?" asked Ted.

When Stewart had moved into his office, he'd hung a picture of a saltwater crocodile jumping several feet out of the water, tearing its teeth into a gazelle mid-leap across a river. Ted always liked to look at it when he visited, and this day was no different.

"Not too bad, I'd say," said Stewart. He and Ted had not yet played their game of golf. Stewart was just going to mention this when Ted began to speak.

"And how is Kyle?"

"Excellent, sir."

"You're not too overwhelmed by your new responsibilities, are you?"

Stewart gave him a quizzical look. He had, up to that point, been feeling underwhelmed by his new position.

"Oh, it's nothing, really," replied Ted, still gazing at the portrait. "It's just that we received a few reports from this division about miscalculations."

Stewart felt like he'd been punched in the gut. Bad numbers were neither synonymous to golf with Ted nor to career advancement.

"Don't worry, Stew," consoled Ted. "I made my fair share of mistakes when I first started." Ted paused and chuckled to himself. "Hell, I admit, I still have my fair share."

Stewart nodded.

"No worries, Stewart," said Ted as he walked toward the office door. "We have the utmost faith in you. I mean with a crocodile like Kyle, how could you not be unstoppable?"

Stewart was distraught. This was bad. He'd never before overlooked a miscalculation. He spent the remainder of his day pouring over numbers and making sure everything was correct. Late in the afternoon, he texted Janet to tell her that it would be very late before he got home.

He got a text back from her telling him not to worry; her parents were having a dinner party, she had taken Kyle out to see them, things were going well, and everybody just adored Kyle.

At home, he found that she and Kyle still hadn't gotten back yet. It was 10:00 p.m., and the only other living thing in the apartment was the pig.

Porky followed him into the bedroom and stared at him while he undressed. This was disconcerting. This pig's eyes held a strange intensity. For Stewart, it was as though the pig could not only read his thoughts, but also that it considered those thoughts to be trivial. He threw his socks at the pig, but they curved wide left, and the pig seemed not to care.

"Is there something I can do for you?" he asked the pig, exasperated.

It oinked.

Too exhausted to wait for his wife to come home, Stewart fell asleep on the recliner in the living room, watching the news, as the pig sat across from him, watching him.

***

"Janet, I don't like the pig running around the apartment," said Stewart. When he woke up earlier that morning, he could smell the scent of truffles and green peppers being cooked into an omelet along with what smelled like country apple ham.

When Stewart sat down for breakfast, Janet brought him a cup of coffee, a peeled orange, and some toast.

"No eggs today," she said as Stewart looked dispassionately at his toast. "I used the last of them to make omelets for Kyle and Porky. You should have seen Kyle yesterday. Everybody loves him."

Yesterday, Janet had brought Kyle to racquetball. The day before, she brought it to her bridge club. Today, she was taking it out again. She'd been spending a lot more time socializing lately, and Stewart didn't really mind.

There was still the problem with the pig, though. He'd been spending way too much time alone with that unnerving pig. All it did was stare at him with its cool pig gaze. Nor did Stewart like the fact that Kyle and what was supposed to be Kyle's food were eating truffle, green pepper, and country apple ham omelets when that particular omelet was, in fact, his favorite.

The pig was hunkered in the corner of the kitchen. It noticed Stewart watching him, and it oinked.

"Why don't you take Porky with you today?" asked Stewart.

Janet laughed loudly, then said, "Bring a pig...to the country club?"

Stewart decided to pretend he wasn't being mocked. "Hey," he asked, "could you make sure to pick up some Rocky Road today? We're out again."

At his office, Stewart made certain his numbers were in order. There had not been a single error since he started staying late every day. He almost wanted to run up to Ted's office for affirmation, but decided to take a more professional route.

He opened the intercom to his secretary.

"Have you been able to contact Ted about our golf game yet?" Stewart peered across his office to where his gazelle picture hung and thought what a golf game could mean for him at this company.

His thoughts were interrupted by his secretary saying that, no, Ted was not available this week.

Stewart asked his secretary to try and schedule golf for the coming week. Then, he spent the rest of his day making his numbers perfect before leaving the office.

Reptiles in Tijuana

When Stewart got home, the pig, as usual, was waiting for him at the door. It stared at him accusingly while he made a ham sandwich. It stared at him even more accusingly while he ate the ham sandwich. Stewart felt no remorse.

Janet was still not back. It was possible she was at the country club, but by this hour, only the bar would be open, and it was bad form for a married woman to sit alone at a bar this late into the evening. Stewart figured she'd probably taken Kyle to some party but was annoyed she forgot to tell him. She'd been forgetting a lot lately.

Stewart looked in the freezer and was unsurprised that his wife had again forgotten to pick up his ice cream.

Porky sat on its rump in the middle of the room, its eyes methodically tracking Stewart's movements. A walk to the corner store suddenly seemed like a good idea.

Thoughts of delicious Rocky Road ice cream filled his mind as he walked past Le Che La Rue.

Something familiar caught the corner of his vision, and he noticed his wife sitting at a table by the window. Across the table was Kyle. The head of the crocodile rested on the chair beside Janet, and the rest of its awesome body snaked across the aisles and under the tables of several other customers.

Janet was talking to some patrons at the table across from hers. He figured she must be discussing Kyle because she kept motioning to the large crocodile next to her that had just finished eating its foie gras and was now beginning on a plate of roast duck.

Several other patrons looked in their direction and must have also been enamored with Kyle because they all appeared to smile, laugh, point, and comment when Kyle blinked both sets of eyelids.

Stewart turned around and went back to his apartment. The pig oinked at him as he walked into the door, but he paid no attention.

Why hadn't she told him where she was going? She knew he'd been dreaming about going to Le Che La Rue for years. He would have been excited to hear she'd finally been able to make successful reservations. He would have even made a point to take off work and come along if she'd asked him.

Stewart went to the kitchen and poured himself a whiskey. If the pig noticed Stewart's distress, it didn't show when he gave it the kind of look one might find a mother giving a child after he just colored on a wall with crayon. Stewart sat on a recliner in the living room and wished he had some ice cream. It was three in the morning when he fell asleep.

***

The sun was peeking through the apartment windows when Kyle and Janet walked in.

"Where were you last night?" Stewart asked, rubbing his eyes and walking toward the kitchen to fix himself a pot of coffee.

"I took Kyle to the country club, then I took him to the spa, then we went to Le Che La Rue for dinner, and then we went clubbing." The energy in Janet's smile was too much for this early in the morning. She was glowing.

"You went clubbing? What time did you get home?"

"Oh, Stewart, we're just getting home now. We fell asleep at the afterparty."

Stewart frowned and waited for an explanation.

Janet shrugged. "So I was out all night, so what? You should be thanking me, Stewart. It was all I could do to keep the women off Kyle."

"What?"

"I had to stake him out, you know. Let the all the other ladies know that he was mine." Janet stuck her arms out and shuffled her feet from right to left like a defender in basketball.

Stewart couldn't remember his wife showing this much spunk since well before they'd been married. He curmudgeonly sipped his coffee.

"Oh, Stewie, it's just a little fun. We wouldn't have seen each other until morning, anyway." Janet paused, "Oh, and I told Ted he could take Kyle for a few days."

Stewart began to mention that Ted was snubbing their golf outing, and he probably didn't deserve to take Kyle for a few days, but Janet cut him off.

"I know what you're going to say. Ted's got his own reptiles. Well he doesn't, actually, frogs are amphibians, and everybody knows he doesn't like them and only got them because Marge wanted them. Let the man have a real lizard for a little while."

"Crocodiles aren't lizards," said Stewart, correcting her. "That's like saying a monitor lizard is a crocodile."

"What's that have to do with Ted?"

Stewart suppressed his anger. She was right. It was nothing for Stewart to share Kyle. Sure, he hadn't been able to spend any real time with the reptile of his dreams, but it was OK, it would raise his esteem in the eyes of Ted.

Stewart got it all straight in his mind on the way to his office. He would talk to Janet about spending more time together. Maybe taking a vacation would help rekindle the fire between them.

At work, he asked his secretary if his good friend and boss had gotten back to him about the golf outing.

No, he hadn't.

Important business to be sure. Ted probably just wanted to impress some out-of-town clients. Stewart walked over to the picture of the doomed gazelle.

Stewart hoped that Ted would have the time to get back to him at some point. If his numbers and his crocodile were any indication of his value, there was no way he could go unnoticed by Ted for long.

He occupied himself with work. The numbers were a good distraction. If he'd ever been good at anything it was numbers. He texted Janet and told her to pick up some ice cream on the way home.

***

"I miss Kyle," Stewart lamented as he lay in bed next to his wife, Janet. This was their last morning without the croc. Ted was due to return the gigantic reptile that day. The pig sat at the foot of the bed.

"I know," said Janet, "which is why we shouldn't lend him out anymore. Ted's got plenty of amphibians that he can impress his clients with. You know that he's got a toad..."

"I know," Stewart was irritated. "Everybody knows about Ted's tripping toad." He paused. "And wasn't it your idea to lend him Kyle in the first place?"

"Stewart," said Janet, changing the subject. "I've got something I need to talk to you about."

Stewart did not like the sound of this.

"We need to get another bed."

Stewart looked down at their comforter. "What?" he asked. "What's wrong with this one?"

"Since you've been working nights lately and usually falling asleep on the recliner, I've taken to sleeping next to Kyle, and I think we should get another bed before we get him back."

"What?"

"He's quite cuddly, you know."

Stewart didn't know. Stewart hadn't been able to spend more than twenty uninterrupted minutes with his crocodile since he bought him. "I don't understand why giving Kyle his own bed would help him sleep."

Janet gave him a tentative frown, "The bed isn't for him, Stewart. It's for you."

Stewart didn't even get a chance to say "what?"

"It's really no big deal. We've pretty much been doing it already." Janet seemed to notice the distress in Stewart's eyes. Her face softened, she put her hand on his arm, leaned over, and kissed his lips. It felt good.

"Just try it for one night. If you don't like it, then we can figure something else out." Janet looked at her husband with a softness he hadn't remembered seeing since early in their marriage.

***

The next evening, Stewart was driving home in a cloud of frustration and anger.

Stewart had called his secretary earlier that day when he first arrived to his office. She reported that there was still no appointment for golf with Ted.

At the time, he had figured it was fine. Respect was the name of the game. At least now he knew he had some leverage because it would only be a matter of time before Ted was calling up to borrow Kyle again.

Stewart had been surprised when, a few moments later, Ted walked right in.

"You've got a mighty fine crocodile there, Stewart," Ted had said. He stared at the picture of the doomed gazelle as he always did. "I'll probably need to borrow him again soon."

"Sure." Stewart paused, knowing this was the time to make his move. "Say, maybe we could talk about it when we go out for our golf game."

"I can't do it this week," said Ted. His lips spread into a thin smile as he studied the picture, "I'm going on vacation to Mexico." On this day, the gazelle looked especially helpless.

"Why not next week?" asked Stewart.

"No need to make immediate plans. Just make sure you keep in contact with my secretary."

Stewart had said nothing as Ted left. He couldn't believe the nerve of the man. He'd been calling Ted's secretary for weeks, and it had never got him anywhere. The message was obvious. Ted was blowing him off again. There was never going to be golf.

Reptiles in Tijuana

Now his drive home was filled with numerous fevered attempts to call Janet, who wasn't picking up, to vent his many frustrations about Ted and his job. It didn't matter. He almost didn't want to talk to her until he was able to sit down and tell her the whole story uninterrupted, while eating a bowl of ice cream.

Hopefully, they would be able to come up with some reasonable solution to his problems with Ted. He remembered a time in his life when nothing was more consoling than Janet and a bowl of Rocky Road.

When he arrived home, there was a note on the apartment door.

Stewart,

I've been rather stressed lately and decided to take a vacation. For the next couple of weeks, I will be sunning myself in beautiful Tijuana, Mexico. Don't worry, I've taken Kyle with me because I think he's also getting stressed, and I feel the tropical air could do him some good. We'll send you a postcard when we get there.

I hope everything is going well at work,

Janet

P.S. Don't forget to feed Porky.

Stewart dropped the note on the ground, believing the news could not have come at a worse possible time. He needed her now. He needed Kyle, too.

Didn't she care about him anymore? Was Kyle the only reason she was still with him?

He sulked into his apartment and walked into his kitchen to get some ice cream.

In the kitchen, both the freezer and refrigerator doors were open, and the floor was strewn with vegetables, condiment bottles, and bags of fish sticks. And there was Porky, sitting between the refrigerator and the counter on its big old pig rump in the middle of its makeshift pigsty. Its snout covered in what looked to be ice cream.

Next to Porky was an empty container of Rocky Road. The pig stared up at him with what looked like a satisfied smile, like a bully high on a power trip. It oinked.

For a moment, Stewart thought about how nice it would have been to have the sun on his skin had he been soaking up rays on a beach in Tijuana.

"That's my Rocky Road!" screamed Stewart. He wondered if he still had a wife, if he should go after her, if he should even care anymore. He wondered if all the work he'd done in his life had been for nothing.

He looked down at Porky, sitting on the tile floor and staring blankly up at him as it always did.

"I've had just about enough of you!"

Stewart grabbed a butcher knife from the counter and launched himself at the pig.

Porky squealed while scrambling around to the other side of the counter. Then it ran across the hall into the living room. Stewart ran after the pig and positioned himself so that the study was the only direction the pig could flee. As he closed in on the pig, that is where the pig went, splashing into the pool of muddy saltwater.

Stewart walked in slowly and closed the door behind him.

Reptiles in Tijuana

"Let me tell you something, Porky," said Stewart as he raised his knife and looked into the eyes of the terrified pig. "If nobody else is gonna eat you, I will."

About the Author

Saul Lemerond was born and raised in Green Bay, Wisconsin. He currently lives in Mount Pleasant, Michigan. His work has appeared in *Dunesteef, Temenos, The Drabblecast*, and various other journals. He hopes someday to move south because his hands get cold in winter.

Also from
One Wet Shoe Publishing

Cuttyhunk: Life on the Rock by Margo Solod.
Paper, 298 pp., $19.95, plus s&h.
ISBN 978-0-615485-39-3

For a complete listing of One Wet Shoe Media
publications, please visit our website at
www.onewetshoe.com. Books and e-books can be
ordered direct from our website with secure
on-line payment using PayPal, or by mail
(check or money order).